Baby Remember
My Name

Baby Remember My Name

An Anthology of New Queer Girl Writing

Edited by
Michelle Tea

CARROLL & GRAF PUBLISHERS
NEW YORK

BABY REMEMBER MY NAME
An Anthology of New Queer Girl Writing

Carroll & Graf Publishers
An Imprint of Avalon Publishing Group, Inc.
245 West 17th Street
11th Floor
New York, NY 10011

AVALON
publishing group incorporated

First Carroll & Graf edition 2007

ISBN-13: 978-0-78671-792-7
ISBN-10: 0-7867-1792-0

9 8 7 6 5 4 3 2 1

Book design by *Ivelisse Robles Marrero*
Printed in the United States of America
Distributed by Publishers Group West

Contents

Introduction

Just now I was downstairs at this Italian place eating chicken parmigiana and a song from My Bloody Valentine's *Loveless* came on. It was one of those times where you catch a shred of a song and it sort of knocks you sidelong into a body memory. For a weird and confusing second, you're *there*. Where I was was twenty-three, maybe twenty-four years old. I was walking through the streets at night, alone, and there was noise and spots of light all around me and I pushed forward, through it. Or I was in my room, which was just filthy, clothes everywhere, stacks of paper so tall they slid out the window, glass candles from the Mexican markets burning on the floor. It was always nighttime in my twenties, or at least that's how I remember it. It was always dark, the lights low, and I never liked my clothes as much as I wanted to, I just couldn't get it *right*, and I was always alone and wanting to be with some girl who didn't want me. Except when I was with a girl and wanting to be alone again, wandering the streets with the only person who truly understood me, myself.

I hate to become the sort of person who talks about how once they were young and now they're not. It's so boring, and relative besides. But still, how strange to get bonked by a song and realize that there was this place you once were, a geography as physical as any alleyway, your twenties—your *youth,* man—and you just aren't there anymore. All the girls in this book are there right now. It's so exciting. I'm rooting for the bunch of them—on their lonely drug adventures, wondering melancholy about girls they left behind as they moved deeper into their wild queer lives, getting their hearts cracked, tripping on childhood, trying to figure out how they're going to pay rent. Not that all of these stories are true. I know a lot of them are chock-full of lies, or wishes, or pared down to the sharp edge of reality good fiction cuts you with. These writers are tough and strong and funny, and their work takes risks that look effortless. They land on their feet or they get scraped up, and either way it's gorgeous. I am so unbelievably psyched to get to work with them, and you are so unbelievably psyched to get to read them. Enjoy.

Michelle Tea
San Francisco
August 2006

Acknowledgments

The editor would like to thank everyone who always points her in the direction of awesome new writers she hasn't met yet, including Sara Seinberg, Anna Joy Springer, Heather Woodard, Rocco Kayiatos, Don Weise, Tara Hardy, and Eileen Myles. Extra thanks to Don Weise for such a great opportunity, and to Rocco Kayiatos, for looking so good.

Keep Your Goals Abstract

Page McBee

This is what I look like: flat. Glowing. My heart and teeth rattle in the wind. It is January, and there are ice storms clotting Texas. I am moving to California as we speak. Time distends. I don't know what to think about besides the weather and the fucked-up geography.

Jim and Kate's Wedding, Buffalo. Disposable Camera.
January 5.

I am home, postcollege, listless. Jim and Kate have been together since high school and they look it—puffier versions of their former selves. Their wedding is a who's who of everyone I could give a shit about. This one girl whose name I forget keeps trying to kiss me. I think we had Earth Science together in the tenth grade. She left Buffalo and then came back, too. I don't know what I'm doing here, but I know I'm not going to make out with some girl whose name I can't remember. I drink cocktails out of heavy glasses and realize I want to leave but can't think of anywhere to go but home. I am red faced and surly. Someone's arm is around me, a big guy with a kid and a dumb smile. I liked him over lobster, but not over dessert. Tomorrow my dad will kill himself. I have ring around the collar and my tie is too short. I look ridiculous.

Mom in front of house. Buffalo. Polaroid. January 9.

Grandma is moving back in, and that's my cue to leave. Dad's blood isn't even really scrubbed off the sidewalk. Such a showboat, to the end. My heart fucking breaks. What was he so sad about? Just yesterday he tried to get me to eat cereal with him. *Buddy,* he said with his trademark false camaraderie, *something just doesn't seem right between us.* I said I was busy. It goes to show you, you never know when you'll only have a grave to talk to.

In this picture, Mom doesn't know where to put her hands but she looks good. That day, I spent all morning in bed with a hangover from that ridiculous wedding, so I'm the one who heard the shot. The trees rustled and I looked out the window and saw him there. I called 911 because I'm an idiot. People who shoot themselves in the head don't need ambulances. I think the dog tried to eat him, but I'm not sure. She snapped at his face. I covered him up with his jacket, not mine.

The funeral was surreal. So many people I've never met shaking my hand solemnly. Jack Fordsman really liked my tie. He made a big deal out of it while we were eating fancy cheese at my house afterward. His face was dry, and he looked old. He'd been my dad's coworker for twenty years, and he seemed really scared. We're all too young to die. I would have been comforting, but fuck him. At the funeral, Uncle George got really heavy handed with the eulogy. He stood, long-bearded and tattooed, and called my dad an *Angel*. Grandma beamed with her eyes, and Mom was checked out entirely next to me. Everybody is so full of shit.

I found this camera in the hallway closet. It's from the '70s, dusty. My heart is anxious, fluttering in my ears. I feel sick. Mom tries to get me to take Dad's sweaters but I won't. I don't want to remember him. It's freezing here. Mom barely looks alive. Every part of her face looks tight and the light on her is dull. I miss her already.

Blur out the window. Central Ohio, dusk. Polaroid.
January 11.

So I don't know if Parker really understands that I'm coming out to California. She's only just moved there, and I've never left the East Coast before. She used to make fun of me for that back in Boston. I called her from our foyer a few hours ago, the echo of my own voice spinning in my ear. I said: *My dad is dead and I need a change already.* She seemed a little stunned, but you can only tell someone you're in love with them so many times before they get it. That's my personal proverb. In college, we even lived together. Parker would make the whole house smell like the seasons—something about the candles or the hot cider or the cinnamon. She used to lie on our hammock and sleep late into the night. She says, *Benji—you do what you need to do.* Her bones are like waterfalls and she's seen me cry.

Ohio is ugly out the window. Desolate, like something lost. People live here, it's mind blowing. What do they do for fun? This is what I've eaten today: chips, soda, and a nasty burrito from 7-Eleven. Road food curls itself up like an animal in my belly. I passed a genuine roadside phone booth a little bit ago. I pulled over, but then couldn't think of what I'd say to anyone I called, and then I wondered about why the shoulder of the road is called the *shoulder.* Either way, it was a soothing place to cry.

Me, haggard and fucking cold with foggy glasses. Taken by another tourist outside of the Sears Tower. Chicago. Polaroid. January 13.

Parker didn't like my dad. They only met briefly, junior year, and he creeped her out. When he drank too much sometimes he'd tell dirty jokes in really inappropriate situations, like dinner at a nice place with a white tablecloth in the North Shore. I called her today and she said I make her nervous. Then she smiled with her voice. I didn't bring enough clothes with me. I didn't bring enough anything. The roads are icy. I'm going South. I'm buying an atlas. When I told her I was in love with her again today, she said, *Why haven't you ever said anything? I'm in love with you, too.* It's weird how we all can speak the same language and so rarely understand each other. Sometimes I feel like I can't breathe. I can't wait for the ocean air. The giant squid has eyes the size of dinner plates. Parker's eyes are like that, and blue like the earth from space. Once we got wasted and went dancing at this stupid club with a bunch of kids I barely knew and I almost kissed her, but I was drunk and she was composed in her cowboy boots. She's the one who told me to *Keep your goals abstract* at that dirty rocker bar in Cambridge when I didn't understand about my life. She would dance alone in her room and I would listen to her late at night. Parker is the best thing in the world to fall asleep to. Chicago burns my ears and it is gorgeous. A homeless lady winked at me and I winked back. Why not?

Waitress at the hipster diner I ate breakfast in, "Mo's."
Little Rock. Polaroid. January 15.

Arkansas is ugly. Last night I stayed at a real shithouse motel. Mom slipped one of Dad's sweaters in my bag, the blue one with little white dots on it. It made me feel really nervous, so I left it in the room. I don't know what the fuck my problem is. Parker was on the beach when I called, and I could hear the wind through her phone. It all made me so jealous. I told her about our trajectory, the growing mythology of my cross-country odyssey, and she got full in her throat. She said to hurry. The waitress keeps flirting with me. I flirt back so I can take her picture when she turns her back and not get kicked out or beat up by her boyfriend, the short-order cook, or whatever. That's a romantic view of a diner. I read too many books. I'm collecting postcards for my mom. I called her to tell her and she didn't have much to say. It's impossible to gauge someone else's feelings. All they did was fight, but she doesn't seem glad to be free of him. I said I'd buy her a plane ticket as soon as I got to the West Coast, even though I don't really want to. I didn't tell her that last part. I'm collecting these Polaroids I'm taking for myself. I think I'd forgotten to look at things. I can't stop looking at bathroom graffiti for signs. This guy in the booth in front of me is yelling at his wife. They're middle aged and he's red in the face. I want to slap him really hard over the head, stun him a little. I wish I wasn't so spineless. I'm not into pissing contests, and I'm not into making a scene. My eggs are cold and not that good. Maybe the waitress's boyfriend is the cook, after all.

Hotel Room, Motel 6, outside of Amarillo, Texas. Polaroid.
January 18.

This room vibrates my nerves until I can hear them ringing in my ears. Last night I had a fucked-up thought before I fell asleep and I couldn't get it out of my head: *Dad hurt me.* I don't even know what it means exactly but I feel fear like cancer crawling through me. My muscles got all tense and then I got worried that someone was murdered in the room. Amarillo is a really shitty town, just a truck stop, basically. Some bad things happened there. I drank a tall boy of Budweiser from the 24-hour gas station across the street, but even that didn't help. I feel like hell today. Parker says I'm repressing a lot of stuff. Lately she talks to me in a really quiet way: not just her voice, but the comfort of her is quiet, too. I like it. She keeps me still. I'm just glad to get out of here. I'm much too skinny to take on these fat asshole Texans at gas stations who look at me and think *fag*. I almost died in an ice storm last night. No one knew how to drive in one. The hotel room had bedsheets from the early '80s. It smelled like cigarettes and other people's bodies. In the morning, I locked up in bed and couldn't move. I didn't snap out of it until I heard the birds on the balcony, screaming at each other. This place is a hellhole.

Somewhere in the Arizona desert, the sparkler in my hand, blurry and bright. Polaroid. January 19.

No joke, the desert at night is cold. I can see every star I looked for as a boy under the heavy industrial skyline. It's like they unfolded for me tonight, a big fucking arrow. I brought gloves and my workman's jacket, but that's not even enough. It's lonely without any trees. I also don't have any cell phone reception. Parker cut her hand when I called, dropping a plate into her soapy sink. I can see it all in my head. She said, *Remember that time we went to that cheesy club a few years ago? I really wanted to kiss you.* I laughed and laughed, it felt so good, and the air was cold. I could feel it coat my lungs. I wish I could call her now. Lately, visions of my death have danced in my head like fucked-up sugarplums. Every childhood fear I never knew I had manifests itself in empty highway hallucinations. The Tin Man chops my mom's head off, the ghost of a little boy follows me with an ice pick, the Boogie Man hides in my closet and looks surprisingly like my father. I try to think about bio-rhythms, the ocean, the prickly hair on my face, and the satisfaction I'll get from shaving when I get there. Home. I don't even know what it looks like.

Stardust Casino bathroom, Las Vegas, myself in mirror.
Polaroid. January 20.

I had to stop at a Wal-Mart in Phoenix this morning to pick up more film. That town is all mud and rainbows. People seemed friendly enough, less swagger than Texas. Still, they didn't smile much, and the kids were chubby. I don't miss my dad at all and it's giving me stomach pains. All I can think about is weird shit, like that one time I found kiddie porn on his computer. I couldn't tell if it was real or not—I mean she could have been a young eighteen but she was dolled up schoolgirl style. It made me sick. I tried to look at him in the face over breakfast the next day and I couldn't. Something cold filled my chest. Parker says I have something heavy to deal with. In college I never wanted to go home, I got really angry about it. My mom would call me about Christmas and I would buck for days. My thoughts move in slow circles, like ice skaters. I drive toward lights.

Vegas is a spectacle. I burned through hours of blank, flat space and then suddenly the city exploded on my windshield. It's tacky and immoral and full of midwestern tourists who look at me with my New York tags and tight jeans and think I know more about city life than them. I look like hell. Too many potato chips, too little sleep. It's 2 A.M. and they've been bringing me gin and tonics for a couple of hours. I deposit quarters deliberately but very slowly into slot machines; I have a whole system worked out. You have to keep playing or they won't serve you, and these are the best cocktails I've ever had. The waitress is on to me, but I've got straight teeth and pretty eyes and I try to charm her into being my reluctant accomplice. The only other people in the casino are old, probably gambling addicts. This one guy keeps begging me for quarters. I've got my hoodie on and my dirty jeans; I guess he thinks I'm an ally. We both need to brush our teeth. We're the lonely hearts club, the off-season, the real losers. I win ten bucks and put it all right back into the void. At 4 A.M., even the waitress leaves for the night. I can't sleep, but I go back to the motel anyway. I do fifty push-ups and one hundred sit-ups. I read yesterday's paper. I fall asleep with all my clothes and the TV on.

The amusement park at the Santa Monica piers, ghostly. Late at night. Polaroid. January 22.

I wasn't ready yet. I called Parker and said I'd need another day to sort things out. In Buffalo, my mom answered on the first ring. She said Dad wasn't my real dad, Uncle George was. Dad knew, he was pissed. Was there anything I wanted to tell her? I felt light-headed, sick. *No, Mom,* I said, *Nothing.* Uncle George spent most of my childhood fucked up on acid, building birdhouses, and tattooing himself in his friends' garages. We hung out occasionally; he took me to a strip joint in high school and I could never decide if I thought he was cool or a total dick. He always seemed like a lesser evil next to my dad, but that's not saying much. My mom cried when she told me, all of that guilt heavy on her like jowls. I wanted to spit through the phone. I'm tired of other people's mistakes.

The ocean is gorgeous, and LA is warm and ugly, just like I expected. Movies really get it right. I went to Hollywood today and it was all maps to stars' homes and Mann's Chinese Theater and cokehead fuckup child actors and the occasional freaked-out movie star. I've never been so happy to be an anonymous guy. I love Santa Monica though, just me and the homeless tonight. I lie on the beach until I get too cold, and I try to empty my mind. It works a little. Parker calls and her voice makes my heart electric. I have sand in my hands and between my teeth. She says she's cleaning her house and changing her sheets. I feel the pages of my life turning, visceral. I put my toes in the water and it is cold. Some things can still surprise me.

Traffic on the 580, outside of San Francisco. My shaking hands and the steering wheel make a cameo. Polaroid. January 23.

The terrain changed. The 5 stunk like slaughtered cows and everything got greener and greener. I can feel the city on the horizon. Rush hour holds me back and my brain spins a little, and then stops. Parker's phone goes straight to voice mail— she's in a tunnel, rushing home on the train. We're playing a game, who will get there first? She always wins. It's raining a little, but I don't need my jacket. The traffic is at a standstill, so I get out of the car. A jammed highway is the least scary place I've ever been. I feel like David and Goliath. I'm hungry, I can taste it, and my stomach somersaults. Parker calls me from her bedroom. *Where are you?* She asks, *Some part of me feels like you've been fucking with me. Did you ever even leave Buffalo?* In response, I hold my phone up in the California air. *Can't you hear it?* I mean my heartbeat, the hot rumble of idling cars, the distant horn honk, the ocean I know that bends ahead. *I hear it,* she answers. My stomach hurts again, and I remember my dad, proud at my high school graduation. He drinks scotch at the party and stares down Sara Crolly's shirt. My mom looks away and I steel my eyes when he shakes my hand. *Congratulations, kid,* he says. He slips me a one hundred dollar bill. The cars start moving and I hop back in the Toyota I've had since high school. Something tastes salty. Maybe it's the sea air. It can't be that much farther from here.

Homo Marriage Redux

Zoe Whittal

Everywhere you go, you look for your narrator, the heroine of your dreams. She's one hopscotch square ahead, changing her hair color, drinking 40s outside the 7-Eleven in a flash of photo-based memory. She was the girl who stepped back laughing while playing the trust game, glint in her thirteen-year-old eyes, like you do when you realize you can question authority and moral of the story and you start to see adults as fallible, objects, objecting, bumps in the log in the bottom of the sea. She studied the curve of your cheekbone, she chose you.

That said, your elusive heroine is otherwise engaged in perpetual adventure. She buys you a pin that says "retired riot girl"; stares at you from a hidden corner of the bus when you talk to your editor on your cell phone, and complain about the constant search. Her eyes are Pop-Tarts half-bites, her tears malleable. She watches as you find yourself at four weddings in a season where the front page of the *Globe and*

Mail shows a Canada engaged in engaging us. She sees you look around the bar at the ocean of twenty-one, twenty-two, twenty-three, maybe.

He thinks if he invites his old revolutionary friends to his wedding that they'll stand awkward in the pews mouthing, class traitor! sell out! conformity! If you really dissolved and resolve, you say to him, mostly we are adults now, with a complex analysis, an understanding that it doesn't always go verse, chorus, verse crescendo, and right back into the way you pictured your life. You hope for interesting, for hot hearts and static fits of passion, the dough rising and falling and pounded by your fists, settling warm in whatever way the building of your body settles and shakes. This is your body to save and cherish, honor, and obey. The best you can do is listen to it, guard it. Take your brain out for drinks, introduce it to your body, and hope they get along. The heart records a mixed tape soundtrack and sets the mood.

I'm trying to find my heroine in a narrative where she is the forgotten en dash in the shadow of the hyphen, the more popular em dash. She's reconciling her rage and daydreams with a fate far more lovesick and brash, she's noting your problems with expectation. She knows you'll never be the one at any altar and notes your hesitation to engage in marital debate.

Reporters have you in their Rolodexes under "lesbian comma artist" and whenever they need one for a quick quote, you get awkward voice mails asking, what do you think should be done about gay marriage? You don't call back because you know the government has a bad track record with love, and that love and taxes make incompatible kissers, and that religion and government should go sit in the coatroom and think about the mistakes they've made. But you have three toes in the real world, watching the boy-choir of lesbos sing "We Belong" by Pat Benatar while two queer girls exchange cupcake-tongued vows, and your heroine watches you cry, because a complex emotion is always a gorgeous one. And in the shadows of right-wing uprising, getting stronger in ways that make you shut the TV off with a cold clammy hand, you tell the reporter that a good thing to do about gay marriage is turn off the radio and ignore the newspapers and volunteer to be a pervy flower girl in a celebration of the excess of love, that you want to be in a room dancing drunk and celebrating anyone who will commit to anything. You say that the construct of love is too messy to pin down, too easy to mock. You are not an earnest love song but you are also no anthem.

You always said you wanted to grow up to be a kneesock or a boxing glove, never a wife.

Your heroine watches you mourn another relationship, she stares at you from the pages of a photo album, asking you to trust your instincts and dare to change. A philosopher tells you the hands are the only visible part of the brain and your brain says to hold tight to the boy you just let go of. She's asking you to ease up on impulsivity; initiating breakups as part of a chemical sideshow, that's her territory now.

But you blink and your heroine is off running, and you're still chasing her streetlight to streetlight, chapter to chapter. Your editor says to make her more believable and she sticks out her tongue. Suddenly she's spitting down on you from an Ossington Street rooftop against a skyline of cerulean and pomegranate, you see HOPE spray painted on these West End walls and she giggles with her hands over another girl in the alley. You think that when you catch her, push her flat against the page, tongue becoming text, taking her revolutionary dreams to heights only hit in art, you'll register at the Pottery Barn when you're novel gets written, take it down the aisle, and celebrate this fiction, because so much of this is.

Juan the Brave

Claudia Rodriguez

It was a hot Saturday morning. While all the kids were indoors eating their bowls of sugary breakfast, Juan rode his tiny blue dirt bike up and down his block. His hair was wet from having showered and he wore his blue Bermuda shorts with the white flower prints. He pedaled faster and bit down hard on his lower lip with each up and down pump of his legs, a sign that he was *echandole ganas a su* bike ride. The ends of his hair curled up toward the sky like light brown hooks. Magdalena, Maggy for short, Doña Rigoberta's youngest daughter, was also outside with her pet Chihuahua, Tito. Maggy watered her mom's rose garden and Tito bit his underbelly where the fleas feasted on him.

"Hi, Erica!" yelled Maggy.

Juan ignored Maggy as he got up from his seat, leaned over the handlebars looking as if he were about to take a plunge into the cement, and leaped off the sidewalk just before reaching Doña Rigoberta's yard. He only soared, at the most, five inches off the ground but imagined himself hovering in the air, doing a complete 360 and landing with the bike tires safely planted on the pavement.

"Ericaaah!" Maggy waved with one hand and held the water hose with the other as a puddle accumulated in the flower beds. "Erica . . . hi."

Juan could spend all day riding his bike from one corner of the block to the other; this was the only route he was allowed to play on. He didn't dare go into the off-limit zones, the always-busy Compton Boulevard, or around the block because his mom would take his bike away—*de castigo*. No one rode their bike more than Juan did. Juan rode his bike because it felt better than cannonballing into a pool on a hot summer day and because no one could tell him what to do while he was on his bike. He could pedal slow, fast, straight, or as crooked as he wanted to. Juan treated his bike the way cowboys in the Western movies he'd seen with his dad treated their horses. Juan had seen more than thirty Westerns with his dad. They would go to the downtown theater, the one that showed only movies from Mexico's golden cinema, to watch an early show. From the entire stock of cowboys Juan liked El Charro de Mexico, Pedro Infante, the most. Not because Pedro would beat up all the bad guys and win the ladies over with his long and soft singing, but because Pedro's mustache was always so neat and thin—perfect like a streak left behind by a bike tire. So Juan rode his bike and that's what he loved to do. He didn't like playing house with the girly-girls because they were too clean and giggled a lot. He didn't really like any of the girls on his block anyway except for Marisol.

Juan thought Marisol was prettier than any woman Pedro Infante charmed and she was only fifteen! Her burgundy hair fell down to the middle of her back, her lips matched the color of her hair, and the oil-black liquid eyeliner she wore gave her brown eyes a sharp slanted look. She wore acrylic nails and a gold ring on each finger and hung out on the street corner or her porch and watched the boys play football and call each other names. Marisol was Joker's *novia* but she still played around with Juan a lot.

"Hey cutie . . . are you still my *novio*? You're so strong." Marisol teased Juan and made him smile. He smiled wide revealing his big front teeth and small gap on his bottom row and his cheeks would get as big as gumdrops. Sometimes he would pop wheelies or do other bike tricks to show Marisol how strong he really was. It tickled a bit inside his ear every time she responded with an *"Ooh, que fuerte eres Juan!"*

"Erica, do you want to play house with me? Let's play that my doll was our baby and that I was watering the vegetables so that I can cook them later and . . . and," Maggy belted out again at Juan.

He slammed hard on his brakes leaving a curvy black streak on the pavement. He kicked his kickstand and slowly leaned the bike on it, not letting go until he was sure that the bike would not fall over. He walked over to Maggy; his hands were akimbo in a cowboy kind of way. The water from the flowerbeds had spilled over onto the sidewalk and Juan's steps made squishy noises as he approached Maggy. Tito bounced up and down almost reaching the top of the fence but Juan wasn't scared. He slapped his hands together making a loud popping sound that sent Tito running inside his doghouse.

"*No me llamo Erica! Me llamo Juan!*" Juan screamed and flipped a curl away from his eyes with a twitch of his head.

"You can pretend *que tu eres el papá* and that the bike was your car to go to work. I won't make you kiss me the way Vanessa makes you kiss her. *Sí* Erica?" Maggy continued to persuade Juan.

"*Te dije que no me llamo Erica!*" He yelled at Maggy. "*Me llamo Juan!*" Juan stomped on a large puddle sending spots of muddy water all over Maggy's pastel yellow coveralls. Maggy's eyes fluttered as she looked at her polka-dotted coveralls and cried. Tito rushed out of his house with his lip snarled and tiny sharp teeth protruding. Juan jumped on his bike and took off as fast as his little legs could take him and left Maggy and Tito behind howling together. Laughing while he sped away, Juan looked occasionally over his shoulder to make sure that Doña Rigoberta or her sons, Paco the one with the shaved head or Joker the one with the scar on his face, were not chasing after him.

"I told you that's not my name," he shouted. Juan, so caught up in yelling, didn't realize he had pedaled all the way up to the intersection of Palm St. and Compton Blvd., the off-limits zone, until he was in the middle of the large street. Traffic was light but a car, with its horn blaring, headed straight toward Juan. He dragged his foot along the cement and gripped his hand brakes making the veins on his hand swell but was not able to stop his bike. There was a long screeching sound punctuated by a loud "pop" as the driver of the car slammed on his brakes and swerved away from Juan and his bike. Half of the car ended up on the sidewalk with a flat tire and inches away from a fire hydrant. In all the commotion, Juan remained glued to his bike seat until his bike hit the curve, jumped onto the sidewalk, and collided against a bus stop bench. The handlebars ended up in the shape of a U and Juan's shoe and pants looked like Tito had chewed on them.

The driver of the vehicle, an older man with glasses, white mustache, and patches of white hair, ran over to Juan. He noticed the tag, with Juan's home address and phone number, on the bike. He picked up Juan along with the curled-up bike and took both of them home.

The driver approached Juan's house. "Ms., is this your daughter?"

Juan's mom who was outside turning the soil and yanking the weeds from her herb patch hadn't noticed the two approaching. She heard the man's voice and turned up from her crouched position. She didn't see much of the man but his mustache and the glare from his glasses.

"*Sí, es mi hija. Qué pasó, Erica? Estás bien!*" she said, recognizing Juan's shoe. Juan's mother's face turned yellow at the sight of Juan with his messy hair, ripped pants, and smudged face. She didn't even get up; she walked on her knees over to where the man put Juan down and wrapped her arms around him, burying his entire face in her meaty bosom. She cried and rocked side to side with her child. Meanwhile, Juan with his one good shoe scratched at the trail of blood that trickled down his leg. Juan's mom thanked the gentleman, over and over, before she swept Juan up and went inside. The pretzeled bike remained outside slopped against the steps.

Juan didn't go outside for the rest of that day. Occasionally he'd stare out the window at the kids running after each other but was not allowed to go out and play. Some of the neighborhood kids believed Juan refused to go out and play because he was scared to be outside without his bike—his second pair of legs. Some kids believed that Juan's mom was really mean and as punishment she was going to keep Juan locked up forever until his skin turned pale and he could no longer stand the sunlight. Others swore Maggy's brothers, Paco and Joker, beat Juan up and broke both of his legs. Juan had no choice but to stay indoors. Olivia, who was older than Juan by two years, told everyone that Juan *could* go out, he just didn't want to. All Juan did was stay in his room and look at pictures of bikes in the store catalogs. No one ever found out what the real story was behind Juan's decision to quit hanging out with the rest of the kids. Perhaps Juan would have preferred any of the other kids' versions than the truth.

It was a Saturday evening, the sun was setting, kids sat on front steps of their homes or the curb, coming down from the excitement of the day. One by one Juan's family walked out of their house—Sofia, his mom, and Olivia were the first ones out; the last ones out were Juan's dad, because he had to lock the doors, with Juan in tow. All the kids turned around to stare at Juan, not because he was holding a present almost as big as him with a bow that covered his whole face, but because he was wearing a frilly dress. Juan's pink, bell-shaped dress was outlined with white lace and speckled with tiny Stargazers which matched the flower barrettes that pinned his curls down. The dress was a hand-me-down from his sister and made Juan look like a mini-woman. Like one of those dolls that stand on top of wedding cakes. Marisol, who was also outside talking to a circle of guy friends, noticed as the box floated by. Some of the guys pointed at Juan and snickered.

"She's actually wearing girl clothes!" Paco high-fived Joker.

Juan didn't turn around to look at anybody nor did he say anything; he walked on carrying the huge box and stumbled a bit when the layers of the dress bunched up between his legs. Marisol broke away from her circle of admirers and walked over to Juan. She looked over her shoulder at the group of boys, Joker and Paco especially, and pressed a stiff finger to her lips commanding the snickering boys to hush.

"Hi, Juan," said Marisol, her voice bubbly with laughter.

"Leave me alone!" Juan mumbled from behind the bow.

"Where are you going in your pretty dress?" asked Marisol.

Juan looked at the group of boys who continued to laugh and point at him then gave Marisol a look that seemed too grown for his seven-year-old face to make.

"Don't listen to them, they're stupid," replied Marisol nervously. "You look pretty," she added as she slackened her smirk.

"Erica, let's go." Juan's dad jingled his keys for him to hurry up.

"Juan, I still think you're brave," said Marisol in the loopy voice she used when she played with Juan. Juan gave Marisol a quick look from behind the bow, hoisted the box higher, and swaggered awkwardly to catch up with his dad.

Juan and Carlo sat on the curb. Their faces were red like tomatoes from racing to El Janitzio and back. They loved going to El Janitzio the restaurant/bar/candy store because it had a larger collection of candy than the ice-cream trucks that drove down Culver Avenue. They bought candy with the money they got from their moms after many *"Please, no más una cora, sí, Mom?"* Carlo was Juan's next-door neighbor and, when not mad at each other, his best friend. Carlo was ten months older than Juan but two whole sticks of gum shorter. It's true—the marks on the granado tree from the time the boys measured themselves proved it. Juan was not an unusually tall kid but Carlo was short, shorter than all the boys his age.

The two kids sat quietly, the afternoon sun a bright halo behind them as they sucked and licked away at their treats. Juan licked away at the nose of his Pink Panther pop with yellow gumball eyes and Carlo smiled a numb-purple smile from his red, white, and blue American Bomb Pop. Their knees were smudged with gray lines of dirt and sweat. Juan also had pink streaks sliding down his knee into his sock and Carlo had a blue trail cause he couldn't eat the blue stripe from the American Bomb Pop fast enough. Juan shooed away a fly that tickled at his elbow and handed Carlo one of his Pink Panther pop's yellow gumball eyes. They chewed the gum fast to see who could make the biggest bubble. Carlo puffed and puffed, making his face redder, and when the bubble exploded all over his face it turned Carlo's face yellow. Juan laughed and pointed at him. Carlo took his gum and rubbed it over his face like an eraser then put the gum back in his mouth.

"Eeeww, that's nasty!" Juan screamed.

"What? It's my gum!" replied Carlo in between hard chomps.

"Yeah, but now you ate the dirtiness off your face." Juan laughed and mocked Carlo.

"What! It's not that funny."

"Ja-ja-ja!" replied Juan and pointed at the remaining dingy yellow specks on Carlo's brow.

Juan laughed so hard spit clung to his chin, thin and shiny like a spider web. He continued to laugh and point while Carlo rubbed his hand across his face in an attempt to clean off the gum all the while asking Juan not to laugh at him.

"So! At least I don't have a boy's name!" Carlo yelled and stuck his tongue out at Juan.

"Yes you do. . . . CARLO!" Juan screamed loud and big, exposing his pink tongue.

"You know what I mean. Don't laugh at me anymore!"

Juan stopped laughing and looped his gum around his index finger while Carlo continued to pick at his face. Carlo turned away from Juan and they both stared toward the corner, where the sound of loose change was coming from. It was the sound of the Elote Man as he approached with his shopping cart topped with a huge pot of steamed corn, mayonnaise jar, cheese grounds, and a giant bottle of Tapatio sauce. The Elote Man tooted his horn as he wobbled his shopping cart down the street. People turned up from the hoods of their cars, looked up from their newspapers, or stopped in the middle of throwing their football, but no one bought an *elote* from the Elote Man.

Carlo turned toward Juan and asked with a squinty look, "Did I get all the gum off my face?"

"You still have some right there," Juan said as he reached for the fleck of gum on the left side of Carlo's face.

"Juan, why do you say your name is Juan?"

Juan stood quiet for a while. He rolled the fleck of gum in between his index finger and thumb and finally said, "I just like it that's all," then flicked the gum into the air.

"But you're a girl. And your family calls you Erica— everyone at school, a lot of people call you Erica."

"So! You have an uncle that your family calls Lupe. . . . Isn't *that* a girl's name?" Juan got in Carlo's face.

"Yeah, but he was born on December 12, the same day as La Virgen de Guadalupe so he has to have that name. Everybody calls him Lupe 'cause that's his nickname."

"And why does he paint his fingernails for?"

"He doesn't paint his fingernails you liar!"

"Uh-huh! I saw he had them painted at your sister's birthday party." Juan pointed his finger at Carlo as if daring him to call him a liar again.

"Uhm, I don't know. . . . Maybe he wants to have his nails shiny so they can match the *Virgen*'s robe?"

"*Ey! Señor* come back!" Joker yelled from across the street for the Elote Man to stop.

The two kids watched as Marisol and Joker walked hand in hand toward the Elote Man. The Elote Man took the lid off the pot to grab a corn and a cloud of steam shot out like a geyser. The Elote Man stuck a stick through the bottom of the cob, brushed some butter, and smeared a little mayonnaise and then a layer of Mexican cheese crumbs on the corn before he handed it to Marisol. She took the corn and fed Joker the first bite; they both laughed at Joker's smeared mouth. Marisol laughed with Joker the way that she laughed with Juan, or did she laugh that way with everyone? Juan couldn't tell because every time Marisol laughed and smiled he felt it was only for him.

"This one here with the star, this one represents you," Marisol once told Juan as she pointed to the shiny little silver star on the tip of her pinky acrylic nail. Every time he saw Marisol smile Juan felt shiny, beautiful like the tiny star. But now, seeing Marisol laugh that way with Joker only made Juan's face feel hot.

Carlo waited till the Elote Man was way down the street before asking Juan, "Do you want to be a boy? All the things you like to do are boy things."

"It's fun to run and get dirty. Doesn't your sister ever get dirty?" Juan asked still looking at Marisol and Joker share the corn.

"She doesn't now"—Carlo shook his head thinking—"and I've never seen any pictures of her where her clothes are dirty the way yours get."

"Olivia doesn't get dirty either. But I think the things I do are funner—that's why she's such a meanie!"

Carlos shrugged and licked the sticky drops of Bomb Pop off the popsicle stick and Juan looked down at his bony knee and scratched at one of his scabs with a dirty fingernail.

"I just like Juan, that's all. I'm gonna go inside, it's too hot out here."

Later that night Juan took his washcloth and scrubbed away at his dirty knees. He scrubbed and scrubbed until soft red *manchas* replaced each gray streak on his legs. He didn't stop until the red *manchas* stung as the chilly air hit them, then he slid into the still, flat water. His nose and mouth barely poked out of the water as his tiny body glided on the slippery surface of the tub. His *rizos*, color *castaña*, floated like tentacles, crashed then bounced off each other. The sound of the water gurgled in his ears and his red toy sailboat ran into his nose then slowly sunk on its side.

"Juan!" Juan blurted out.

"Bluuh!" he heard between his submerged ears.

Juan stayed in the bathwater until his tiny body felt chilled. When he finally got out the tub, the flat bubbles swirled in the water, now gray from the soap and Juan's residue. He patted himself dry with a towel rough and warm from being dried out in the sun. He got up on the toilet and sat his bare bottom on the cold sink, took his pruned finger, and traced a shaky J-U-A-N on the mirror whose surface looked smeared with tears. As the bathroom got cooler the mirror sweated off all the steam and Juan's face appeared fully on its surface. His lips were violet with chill, his pores at attention, and his hair slicked tight on his head.

"I look like a Juan. I feel like a Juan," he said as he leaned into the mirror steaming it up with his breath, "but I'm Erica." Juan cupped his hand between his legs the way a proper little girl would—the way he'd seen his sister Olivia do all the time. Juan touched his face, admiring it and looking at it for what it was—*una cara de niño*. He noticed than even on his upper lip he had more hair than Olivia. The hair was very small and bent over with softness, but he imagined a mustache thick as grass blades filling in when he got older. He rubbed his index finger over his wet left eyebrow and felt the ridge of his scar. You couldn't really see the scar unless he brushed his eyebrow hair a certain way with his finger. He was too young to remember but his mother told him that he got that scar when he was not even three years old. Juan had tried to crawl out or escape from his crib and fell to the floor cutting his eyebrow open on the foot of the crib. Every time Juan scraped, tore, or blistered his skin, producing blood, his mom would remind him, "*Desde chiquita* you've been this way—never staying or doing what you're supposed to." But Juan didn't consider his *cicatrices* a punishment for being unruly. His cicatrizes were reminders of the first time he popped a wheelie, the first time he jumped or crawled under a fence, the first time he climbed up a tree.

"*Diosito*, did you make a mistake with me? I won't be mad if you did," said Juan as he slid his hands over his chest. He covered his chest the way he did that day at the beach. He was with his three boy cousins—all close in age to Juan and they also looked a lot like him. Juan and his cousins were often mistaken for siblings. His cousins were all boys, all the same size, same short hair that fell like curly fries around their ears and skinny bodies with bellies taut like hot-air balloons. Juan had been playing with his cousins in the hot sand when his cousins decided to take off their shirts. As the boys took off their shirts, Juan noticed another thing he had had in common with his cousins. His chest—it was flat and bony except for two brown spots. Juan, also hot from playing around, took off his shirt soon after his cousins did.

"Sofia! Look at what your daughter is doing," Uncle Beto screamed as he poured more beer onto the *carne asada*. All the kids around stopped building their sandcastles, not sure what Uncle Beto was yelling about.

"Ay Erica, don't be silly, you can't be out like this," said Sofia as she struggled to put Juan's shirt back on. Uncle Beto's words made Juan sting all over while his shirt, all covered with sand, felt like loofah on his skin. Juan wanted to cry under the weight of his feelings—tender like sunburnt skin. But Juan didn't cry because cowboys don't cry. Even when the tears stung his eyes like seawater he still didn't cry. If only Juan could've transformed himself into anything at that moment, he would've turned into a sand dollar and burrowed into the wet sand.

Back in his bathroom he wondered if anyone ever asked Carlo why he, Carlo, liked to do the things he did. Juan felt as if Carlo just did what he liked. When Carlo wanted to scratch he did; *"no te toques ayi" gritaba* Sofia if she ever saw Juan scratching his *cosita*. When Carlo want to spit he did; if he wanted to play ball, ride a bike, climb trees, he did. But people always wanted to know why Juan did the things he enjoyed and was so good at. Adults always asked Juan why he did the things he did except they asked him in a way that, to him, sounded more like they were saying "you're not supposed to like the things you like." Many times Juan felt like an ant under the adults' magnified eye.

"Knock! Knock!"

"Who is it?" Juan got startled by the pounding on the door and wrapped the towel tighter around him.

"Erica, open the door! I have to pee badly and it hurts." Olivia jiggled the doorknob and kicked the door. "Hurry my *panza* is all big."

"Ok, I'm coming."

Olivia banged on the door and chanted "Hurry, Erica, hurry" the whole time it took Juan to get dressed. Juan finally opened the door and saw Olivia standing right in front of the doorway, her legs crossed and mouth puffy with desperation. Even though she screamed that her bladder was stretched to its limits, she no longer twitched as she looked Juan over—not like he was a stranger, but maybe a little bit strange. Juan saw the squint in Olivia's eyes, trying to find something in Juan, but Juan just nudged her out of the way and puffed out his chest like a tiny puffer fish.

Ryan: an excerpt

Amanda Davidson

The sky pushed and pulled, a wet night giving way to a break in clouds, a lessening of darkness, a cessation of rain. Droplets hung on every surface and glittered, as if the matter of the world had jumped (or was about to) and a different set of forms, or possibilities, had been (or was about to be) revealed. A sense of instability whisked about on the chilly breeze.

Ryan and I walked up Parker Street. The acid released tiny waves of calm anticipation in my chest and adrenaline rolled down my guts. We walked briskly, without talking, as if we had a destination. In the empty street a feeling expanded up and out of me, palpable and moist. It roiled between us like hot water. I rowed for a while on a little raft called guilt. It was a familiar accompaniment to any strong, or new, emotion. This time it whorled around a breach of loyalty. Millicent! My friend's name was a shrinking font vanishing on a soaked page, faint, waving for help, blurred, flooded, drowned.

Over the sidewalk, fruit hung on laden branches. Smears of rot and pits, glazed in place, persisted on the rain-soaked cement. I seemed to reach up and detach an orange from an orange tree. I scored the rind with my teeth. The smell made a color in my mind, and I cupped the shredded peels in my palm. They gleamed, ruddy lashes of ochre against the noir backdrop of the neighborhood.

We turned onto the Avenue. It was empty and dark, little closed shops beneath apartments. A bloom hung in the shaken air, and there was Ryan beside me, flushed cheeks and boots. She leaned toward me and spoke in a low hush. "My ex–piano teacher lived on this block."

Ryan looked grim. We stared down the deserted street.

"I haven't walked on this block for months," she said, "not since my last piano lesson, which I never paid for."

A puddle shone on the cracked sidewalk. I stooped to set the peels afloat. We looked up and a lone figure was walking up the sidewalk. Long trench coat, Stetson hat tilted low, trailing smoke from a thin, damp cigarette. Ryan groaned. "That's my piano teacher! Act casual."

We ducked into the doorway of a bike store. Faces pressed to cold plate glass, we window-shopped. Child-sized mannequins rode tiny mountain bikes.

"Expensive presents you outgrow fast," Ryan said. Her dad was rich. Did that make Ryan rich?

The piano teacher's shoes squeaked as he strode by. His flicked cigarette fizzed in the gutter. Nicotine laced the air in his wake. It made me hungry, but not exactly—it sharpened me.

* * *

Now an atmosphere of coincidence whirred at our heads. Down the wet sidewalk we walked and walked. A lustrous gray light began to seep between the clouds. Speech floated around us as small, detached petals twirled groundward. We passed a bakery. Buttery fumes layered the surrounding air. I said, "Long ago, running from one job to the next, very hungry and without money, I entered this bakery. The girl behind the counter gave me samples of every kind of bread, lathered with honey."

Ryan said, "That was me, I worked there."

I began to believe that an angel of coincidence dragged Ryan along in the hem of her robe. Swarms of bees slung down the angel's back were wings, and a buzzing felt along the air indicated her presence. The angel slid her heavy, honey-smelling arms across our shoulders. Large chunks of moving clouds resembled continents breaking apart, and the sky rolled like a wave.

A freeway overpass lay beyond the bakery. Tall abutments streaked with pigeon droppings towered above the stores and houses, a sudden leap in scale. I looked up as we entered its grimy shadow and saw a battered barricade along the freeway's edge. A body would be nothing against that, I thought, a thud, a bag of rocks.

The underpass smelled moldy, rimmed with brine from sewer grates. Frozen escalator stairs led to a gated train station. I was suddenly far away from Ryan, telescoped at the other end of a longing that floated outside of my body and maybe was only attached by a string, not mine, not me. I could walk up the unmoving escalator stairs and wait for the morning's first train to take me back to a familiar place, defined by coldness, where emotions corresponded to known configurations of the body. But, where was that? Maybe I had wandered into an openness from which I'd never find my way back.

We stepped out of the exhaust-streaked shadow of the overpass.

Bewildering rain began to fall.

Before us stood a little flower stand. Cosmos. Under a stiff blue awning, a cedar bench rested against the windowed shop front. The tiny shop was packed with flowers, a thick wave of plant life rolling up to the plate glass. We drifted toward the bench. Drops had blown across the wood. Ryan swept them off with her sleeve, and we clambered up. From under the awning, the world sparkled dirtily. On the narrow bench we sat flank to flank. Ryan's heat seeped through my damp pant leg. A sudden flush pulsed from my clit (DOWN THERE), torrid wave radiating from an inside point to meet the solid press of body warmth from Ryan. Side against side we sat until I couldn't stand it, linked meat vibrating in a continuous field of heat.

I squirmed (or convulsed) and twisted toward the dim interior of the flower shop. A gilt-edged card glinted in a thicket of scab-colored roses. Swooping lamé letters spelled a message: Romantic. I wanted a gesture large and specific, physical. Full throttle tonguing. A sentence wouldn't begin to cohere around it. I tumbled into details.

Gold ink embossed on thick crème paper. The letters had a fuzzy edge. I composed a note for the blank side (nested in petals): Dear Ryan, A pony bucks around within my loins. I feel . . . romantic. Love, A.

Was I at the mercy of larger forces? The moment refused to yield. Rain dripped from the awning's frayed blue edge: Tick.

Ryan grabbed my hand and held it, palm up, splayed, atop her knee. My eyes crossed, or flipped inside out, sight dragged through a tunnel of blood, a scattered shower of platelets rained across the visual field. Ryan dragged a finger tip down my palm and said,
I'm telling your fortune
then I heard: + + + + +
a static-y roar
nothing.

* * *

Clouds evaporated revealing a mindless blue. What had happened? I had dissolved and another thing had formed in place of me. Sunlight warmed the air and the day began to generate a faint, muggy heat. We stopped at the edge of a yard. An unruly garden surrounded a tall clapboard house. Its total enclosure resembled a face. Inside was a family, maybe, as hidden as thoughts. The yard revealed clues: a blue plastic bucket, a trowel, a sodden issue of *Horse Illustrated* magazine.

A picket fence drew a line around the garden.

Mild, blossomy sweetness and a smell of wet dirt rose from the yard. A fat peach rose drooped in the moist grip of air. Each board on the clapboard house radiated in white relief against precise strips of shadow. Objects hummed against the light that shrouded them, as if the stillness contained a potential for reversal. Warmed up, I might dissolve and become a part of the space that kept swallowing me.

Ryan crouched to examine a newspaper. Encased in blue plastic, it rested at the driveway's lip, the edge of the concealed family's territory. She dug into the plastic bag and pulled out a small packet.

"Sunday papers always have free samples," Ryan spit, tearing the little thing open with her teeth and squeezing. A coil of oily lotion glistened on her palm. "Skin polish!" She smiled up at me.

I looked at Ryan; a rip dragged through the blue air between us. A look felt like a touch: rough tongue dragged from gaze to groin. I felt horny and patient. Lust beamed out of my eye and radiated from my pores, forming a haze.

Ryan rubbed her hands together. Wet sparkles glazed her skin. We abandoned the molested newspaper and ambled homeward.

* * *

Sad gargoyles guarded the porch of le Maison, their granite eyes streaked with sloppy applications of paint. Ryan and I trudged up the sticky marble steps. By now the acid had worn off to a cranking subrhythm of cheap speed. It occurred to me that inside the house, waking up, or perhaps not yet asleep, there were people who would look at me, and that when they looked at me they would see me looking at Ryan, and that when I looked at Ryan I revealed something. My bowels rippled in sudden anticipation: a set of perceptions that would collect on my skin. A registry of marking eyes. A peal of exuberance shot through my mind—fuck them!—as we stepped across the splintering threshold.

Fresh smoke curled in the gloomy entryway. In a broken folding chair, smoking and muttering, sat the Phantom. Balding, paunched, of unknown age, the Phantom was rumored to be in the fifteenth year of his undergraduate career. Like me, the Phantom had not yet declared a major. "Bum a smoke?" I asked him.

Looking at the floor, the Phantom held forth a pack of Pall Malls. I extracted a cigarette. Ryan and I headed down the hall. A sticky shuffling was behind us—the Phantom!

In the living room, sunlight streamed through rippled glass windows. Ryan plopped onto a sagging brown love seat and propped a boot atop the dish-stacked coffee table. The Phantom stood in the doorway. His head jerked up, down, sideways, mirroring the sudden drops and dodges of the fruit flies that hovered in the middle of the room. "You guys need any . . . stuff . . . for . . . breakfast?" he asked.

"No, dude."

The Phantom's eyes darted up. Pinned pupils swam in bloodshot jelly. He sighed, lit another Mall, and sank into a couch.

I curled next to Ryan and fixed my gaze on her throat. Coincidence clapped us firmly under her hot wing.

"I'm reading this book—" "*Sexing the Cherry?*"
"How did you know—?" "I am too."

We passed the cigarette back and forth for a while without speaking. Fleshy tugging transubstantiated into smoky lungfuls. I savored proximity and the nasty Pall Mall.

Ryan stubbed the cigarette out and walked over to the piano. I followed her. The Phantom's blunt gaze trailed us across the room. I aimed a hot jet stream of attention at Ryan. Out of tune and missing keys, the piano wobbled as she played. I recognized the damaged melody: George Winston's "Summer." The overly sweet music had formed a soundtrack for my first dry humping episodes with Z, my one and only high school boyfriend, an effeminate bisexual pianist. I stared at Ryan's combat boots pumping the pedals. A little night music rustled in my pants.

Oh Lonely Adventures

Sloane Martin

The guy who sold us acid had lived in the park for six years before he started dealing, and now he had been there for almost forty which he said felt like forever and the place never went back to the way it was during the sixties.

He was burrowed into a little hollow behind some trees just through the tunnel off of Haight Street on the way to the big colorful metal structure of the children's playground. He rustled out and startled us with his voice-scratch, infested with nicotine *Hey. You guys want some acid?* His girlfriend was a mushroom dealer, he told us in polite pre-illicit dealings conversation, and she made more money because she found her shit in the park, didn't have to pay anything for it, paid a friend for a room in an apartment and they wouldn't let him come live with them because he didn't like to bathe very often. To me it smelled like he didn't like to bathe ever, only I didn't say it because I didn't want to offend him and get overcharged since we only had just enough money on us and I'd gone to such elaborate lengths to make sure I wasn't going to go home tripping.

I hadn't ever done acid, which was silly because I'd already done coke and that's way worse so it felt like I had skipped a step on my way up the drug chain. I swore I wouldn't do heroin ever because I had read *Naked Lunch* and that guy was way cracked out but if it wasn't really expensive or if it was right there I would probably do it and then I'd be so far ahead it would be pointless to go back and I'd never get around to doing acid.

The acid guy was really skinny but swollen like he had filled up with air instead and he smoked furiously through a thick fistful of joints he kept fishing out of his pocket and picking through like they were coins, a whole stack of them ready, rolled in his pocket.

Once I got caught smoking at school and had to go to this anti-smoking meeting which was cool because we sat in a big group and you could do whatever you wanted as long as no one could see you and the theater was so dark no one could. Plus I got to miss math. Some of the kids had gotten caught smoking pot, not cigarettes, but they had to go to the meeting too and they were asking the lung lady who came to talk to us all sorts of questions about how many cigarettes equals a bowl and if cold smoke off a bong does the same sort of damage as hot smoke off a cigarette. The lady passed around this jar of molasses that was supposed to symbolize the amount of tar in your body if you smoked a half a pack of cigarettes every day for one year and told us that there was five times as much tar in marijuana as in tobacco and all I could think of was how much tar must be in the acid guy's body if he'd been smoking joints like cigarettes since the Sixties.

The house we went back to was a few blocks away from Haight Street in an area the yuppies called Cole Valley and the hippies called the Upper Haight because they didn't want to be labeled yuppies. The house belonged to this guy whose nickname was Jax because that's what he tagged but I didn't know what his real name was, all I knew was this kid lived in his North Face windbreaker and Diesel jeans and complained how all his money went to spray paint and cigarettes. The air in his room smelled like soapy coffee and hot oranges and the carpet was an ugly green like frozen pizza olives. Jax had a best friend Paul who had a chemical imbalance that made him seriously psycho-crazy-insane-strange and I was happy he wasn't there when we did acid. He had been there when I did mushrooms for the first time and I was so embarrassed, retching and tripping and the room swaying around me as he watched. Instead I was with Sage, my somewhat boyfriend. We hadn't decided what we were yet, it was confusing, having sex but no romance whatsoever. Sometimes I thought maybe I was in love with him and then I would think about what a terrible couple we would be, and even if I did ever have real feelings for him I'd be too afraid of rejection to say it, and the feeling was mutual.

Sage had so much power over people; he didn't even realize it, how badly he could fuck with a person's head if he wanted to. I think it was mostly the fact that he didn't care about many people so everyone wanted to be one of the ones he did care about. I was one. I didn't know what would happen if he wasn't there all of a sudden and I had to stand on my own, but while it lasted I would bask in the security of it.

But the acid. We had a tab each and it took a while so I got bored and went to take a shower and while I was in the tiny glass cubicle the acid hit and I looked around at the water falling and pretty soon the soap I was using had completely disintegrated and I was dripping cold onto the bath mat. Somehow I got dressed and wandered into the room where Sage was stretched out connected to the floor. After a while of us staring at the paint stains in the carpet and the grooves in the wood of the desk, Jax called us. He wasn't home but he gave us a key so we could go when we wanted because his mom didn't care and his dad moved to Mexico or somewhere when he was seven. He told us to come to May's.

May was Jax's girlfriend who was too hot for him although he was pretty hot himself and who broke up with him every four to six weeks. Once they stayed together for three months straight and everyone was waiting for them to break up the entire time and when they finally did we all went and bought a bottle of the worst vodka we knew that tasted like nail polish remover and we gave it to Jax and he finished the whole thing in two days and was still drunk when he woke up the morning of the third. May was nice but fucked up and she didn't know how to deal with her relationship. She had a lot of self-esteem issues even though she was tall and beautiful and had French parents who didn't give a shit what or who she did. She was Euro-gorgeous with big blue eyes and straight blond hair and the kind of acne that was cute because it was just around her mouth in little pink bumps that blended with her freckles. She was tall, but Jax was taller, her beauty enhanced his, and when they stood together it was overwhelming, the beauty that pianoed its way from their bodies and over whoever was with them and made us squirm.

I had a girlfriend once who was like that, who made you nauseous she was so pretty but once I got to know her I realized how she was screwed up inside like the rest of us, and she was crazy not in the way that Paul was crazy, but so she would get in weird moods and have to do things like ask people she didn't know to be her friends or make two dozen muffins and eat them all in one sitting, and that made me feel better since she was earthly and down on my level. I had sex with her in her parents' broken VW bus that was on blocks in her backyard and got rug burns in long pink stripes down my shoulder blades from being pressed so violently into the carpet lining the trunk where we did it, hot and sweatslick and her biting on my neck that made my stomach twist and I ground up hard against her pelvic bone until we were so close our hips were bruising. But May was even prettier and it made me hurt to look at her so I avoided her even though I thought she might really understand me. And I didn't want to go to her house because I was afraid of what might happen if I did.

Sage and I went to my house instead because Sage was sober and I was sobering, and my parents were naïve and gullible enough that we could get away with it. The one time I came home on hallucinogens was when I was on the mushrooms we found in the park and my parents were angry at me anyway and didn't want to deal with me and I just walked upstairs and felt too big for the hallway. I lay down naked in front of my mirror and finally saw myself the way I thought other people saw me and I was tripping still so when I put on music my body moved to it without my realizing it. I lay curled in the dark under my sheets with my headphones as high as they could go and let the heat in the bed build and mingle with the smell of my crotch and felt primal and free. But now here with Sage we lay under the covers together and he smelled so good, sharp and spicy and mingled savory sweet with his cologne like French toast and basil. He touched my leg and I moved it and he said, *I thought that was you, I never felt sheets that soft,* and I smiled and kissed him because he was too nice to kiss me first. I wanted to get it over with because it was such a cliché chick thing but I loved talking to him the best, and post-orgasm conversation is better than pre-orgasm conversation because by that time you've been so close to each other there's nothing you can't say and weird things come up like the sizes of people's genitalia. Once we talked about this guy who used to think he was in love with me who supposedly had a ten-inch dick, his best friend had told us when he masturbated it was like playing a trombone. My house was deep in the middle of nowhere-pastel-cake-stucco land, the Sunset, San Francisco's wastesheet of suburbia, where everything was grungy sun-faded uniform with painted silver gates, long sheets of barred glass, messy garages, and glossy movie posters. When we were done we slunk out of there as fast as we could, horny again, city prowling giving way to excitement and the badass feeling left behind by drugs.

* * *

Sage's entire family knew we were fucking. Along with all of his mother's crazy-creepy friends, two of his father's coworkers, his sister's current boyfriend and her ex, and his brother's therapist. None of them thought it was a bad thing—except the therapist, who had a Freudian take on the whole thing. Sage's parents were free-thinking hippies and his siblings were thirty-ish and long moved out of the house he lived in, a big hollow warehouse downtown that was tall and narrow with at least six floors. It was so cool just to wander around and find things—plants on the elevator, beaded curtains on the bridge, the museum on the second floor full of weird artifacts his parents had found—among them, a can of Campbell's Chicken Noodle soup that had botulism, enough to kill the whole city of San Francisco. But Sage's family was huge, it would take a set of encyclopedias to explain, and every single person in it knew, even his mother's ex-husband who had moved to Japan after the divorce to become a real ninja.

I sat down on Sage's bed upstairs and waited for him to follow after. There was a tingling feeling on the backs of my arms that knew something was happening, or maybe it was the cold. I burrowed under the layers of blankets but the tingle was still there like an almost-itch. Like the time I got poison ivy, it started as just a tingle and bloomed red and oozing into a terrible rash. The pulsing silence was blood-hot, thick and moving under my skin, pulsing and waiting for the tiny cut to let it all out. Sage walked in and looked at me and I could tell he was blazed by the way he shifted, such an antsy stoner, and kept running his hands through his hair.

Do you want to go somewhere? he asked, his voice slow, distracted. This was one of our problems, we could never think of anything to do and usually sat around for a few hours before going at it again. I was determined not to let it happen this time.

Titties at Stake

Dexter Flowers

My first word was *titties,* I swear. The liberation and freedom of tits was always a hard-core value in my household. Free-flowing bosoms blowing in the wind, breasts that had had their bras burned in the flames and have risen from the ashes. I was the child at the naked hot springs flinging off my tie-dye, running around shamelessly in my birthday suit.

As a teenager, my mom always tried to get me to read about the danger of underwire bras—she believed they caused breast cancer. And if I was going to oppress and bind my tits, couldn't I at least wear a sports bra instead?

When I was ten years old, I was convinced I had breast cancer. My teeny-tiny little girl buds were practically nonexistent, but when I felt them they felt unnaturally lumpy. What was wrong with me? I had images of having an operation like Brenda on *90210* had. I remember in the episode she asked, "What does it look like?" referring to the tumor being removed.

"It looks like a little piece of chewing gum," the doctor replied.

I lost sleep. What if I was dying, right at that moment?

My mother tried to assure me that a girl of age ten wasn't likely to get breast cancer. Then my stepmom said, "Maybe it's a cyst." I became so neurotic that they finally took me to see the family doctor. I was a little nervous. My sixteen-year-old stepsister—who talked to me as an equal and always told me more than I should know—once told me that she'd had the doctor check her for breast cancer and it had made her feel dirty, because he was an old man. I had no idea what that meant, except that it sounded freaky.

In the doctor's office I had my stepmom there for support. The checkup was simple. I raised both arms and the doctor poked me with a gloved hand, and said, "No cysts or cancer. She's just startin' to develop. It's a perfectly natural thing."

Backtrack a couple years to when I was in third grade and my mom, me, my current best friend Candy, and her mom, Donna, went to Sizzler for a mom–daughter night out. My mother launched into this story about how her and her friends were in nature, and it was hot, so they went topless. When people passed by, she insisted, no one noticed, because they were so distracted by nature. She went on. "You know, I bet if I flashed my boobs in Sizzler, no one would notice!" She flashed her braless breasts three times, me and my mother laughing hysterically. No one had noticed, like she said!

Donna stood up and yelled, "I can't believe you, Felicity! Flashing your tits in the middle of Sizzler!" She said this incredulously, like it was a bad thing. We left our delicious dinner of fried shrimp, cheese bread, and iceberg lettuce.

"Take a taxi," my mom said, and we drove away.

At some point later, being at all naked was my worst nightmare. The fact that my mother would smuggle two lemons out of a grocery store, placing one under each tit, didn't impress me. "This is the one thing I steal, because they are so overpriced," she'd say.

At the naked hot springs, I no longer ran like a bare-bodied "child of the goddess" with the other pagan children; I sat with baggy tie-dye shirts over my bathing suit, hoping no one would notice that my breasts were growing.

I remember when Terry my stepdad, me, and my mom went to the hot springs for a two-day pagan crafts fair. All the commune kids, mostly in their teens, ran around stark naked. But I just wasn't there anymore.

My breasts were under siege—deep in the abyss, fighting off wandering men-eyes, trying to cultivate some sort of master plan. And they didn't resurface until I was seventeen years old. I had made, like, six or so friends, and was really excited. Unfortunately, some of them lived in San Francisco. They were all queer girls who were vegan activists. There was literature about the awful truths of factory farming all over their houses, and stashed like a necessity in their back-packs. They called themselves militant vegans. How my rainbow-sherbet-eating, fish-sandwich-eating self befriended them is a mystery. Being that I'd nod my head and agree with every political word on veganism that came out of their mouths, I was assumed to be one of them: militant vegans, fighting for the cause, protector of every living thing.

And I ran with it. When we'd all go out to eat, I'd order vegan. At the burrito place, I'd order the tofu burrito—with guacamole instead of cheese, which is what they all ordered—and moan half-hearted sounds of food pleasure in unison with them. I was a liar. I'd worked so hard to come out, only to go in the food closet, betraying everyone, myself included. I finally had some gay friends, and planned on keeping them.

That's the way it was. No meat, dairy, or eggs, to save face, and then excessive compensation when I wasn't in their presence. Like I was rebelling against their subculture normalcy. Salmon egg scrambles with cheese. Or burritos with chicken, sour cream, *and* cheese. Italian sodas, with half and half, *and* whipped cream.

I got a call one day from Lilah, and she told me that she wanted to create a topless march in our tiny, six-block town of Sebastapol. My boobs perked up at this idea. The phone tree circled, and next thing I knew I was sitting in Lilah and Aaliyah's backyard, plotting a town takeover featuring boobs.

We called ourselves BABES: Breast Action Brigade to Eliminate Sexism. We got a good ten people involved in the planning. It was going to be unbelievable. I was pretty nervous about the whole thing, but I saw this as a great opportunity to make a statement. Plus, this was as close as my farm town was coming to riot grrl and I was definitely a wanna-be riot-grrl, set in the wrong city, in the wrong time.

We all sat around with our cropped and dyed mops of baby dyke hair. We planned on baking vegan booby donuts with vegan chocolate nipples. We actually had a boob donut-making party. We also spent a lot of time making protest signs. My favorite was one that made cutouts for someone's boobs to hang over, and it said: THIS IS NOT AN INVITA-TION FOR RAPE.

It was all just so exciting. And the excitement only grew. We all piled into the car once, late at night, and took our shirts off. We then flyered the hell out of downtown Sebastopol and stood topless on the side of the road, holding huge promotional posters reading "Breast Fest 2000." We got horrified looks and a couple of car honks from the passersby. This was a family town. We piled back into the car, me lying across everyone's laps in the backseat, so we could all fit, feeling like bandits in the night.

For a month we ate, slept, and breathed tits. We got a very concerned answering machine message at headquarters from the junior college. A frantic woman's voice came on. "We'd really like to support your event, but I find this impossible because you literally wheat pasted, actually wheat pasted all over the benches and on some walls." She then went on to encourage less rowdy behavior in the future.

I was part of the rebellious vegan militants, and I liked it. I was going to make my mom proud. Tits out, emerged like supernatural ghosts that had lived in the woodwork for a hundred years. But my breasts were also vampires, scared of broad daylight, unsure and more than slightly cowardly. They were used to being covered, sitting on the bus with naked-topped sweaty men, teen shame written all over them, only coming out at night for brief appearances, all alone, with only each other to be witnessed by. All donuts aside, actually going topless was going to be more of a project than I'd expected.

I reached down and felt my stomach, the way it jutted

out—squeezing, not pinching, the flesh, because when you actually aren't thin, pinches don't exist. I remember reading a teen magazine that said if you could "pinch more than an inch" then you were overweight. That is the number one thing I remember from reading that magazine. I still squirm and shiver when I imagine how many girls must have pinched their tummies to see if they possessed the forbidden well-endowed stomach, the awful, gruesome double-inch. After a while, when it's obvious that you're not in the "inch" ballpark anymore, you stop counting and either grow some sort of complex or just get over it. At this point in my life I'd thought I was over it.

I'd been reading fat positive books and zines, actually embracing my body, but there's nothing like a naked festival to dig up your insecurities. It made me question everything.

My stomach went squish squish.

My breasts went droop droop.

I looked in the mirror like I had a narcissistic mental disorder. Here I was, a coordinator of a topless women's march and I was rejecting myself. My anxiety only grew. I called Lila and was like, "I mean, do you think it's a big deal if I keep my shirt on?" It was ridiculous. We both knew it. All this work only to be cheated out of the cause, a simpleton ally, a sideliner. Not a "double-breasted party machine."

I brought my concerns to my best friend Violet, who told me the same thing I already knew—that I just had to do it, flash my jugs downtown. Violet had started feeling severely neglected since I started BABES. We spent every waking hour together and now I was always out at one breast thing or another. I called her the night of the booby donut-making party to tell her I'd completely lost track of time, and wouldn't be hanging out with her after all. She finally lost it. "You never spend any time with me anymore!" Her voice shook, the way it does when someone saves all their resentments quietly, then unleashes them like crusty underwear found underneath the bed.

"I'm gonna take this in the other room," I'd said, seeming stressed out I'm sure. No one seemed to notice, they were all deep-frying vegan dough and laughing, which probably only accentuated Violet's anger—the sounds of girls having the time of their lives pouring into her hot ears. I felt like some guy watching the Super Bowl and Violet was the wife waiting for it to all be over so that I could watch TV with her and trade foot rubs. I told Violet that I was really sorry and that the march was almost here and then things would go back to normal again. I ditched out early and went home to Violet, feeling more codependent than ever.

The day of the march, I locked myself in the bathroom with my mom's acrylic paints and went to town, transforming my breasts into a multicolored union of art. I painted big yellow shooting stars on my chest with rainbow trails that wrapped completely around each boob, leaving only my nipples exposed. This was the way it had to be if I was going to bare all; no one would know the difference, my cop-out would be hidden, buried underneath the paint.

I put on my cutoff workers pants and a tri-stud belt, hiking them over my belly button. The paint led down to my stomach, hiding my stretch marks effectively. Combat boots and a little gel in my bleached and pink hair and I was done.

I walked out to Violet, who was coming to the demonstration. She was waiting for me in the living room. "Whoa," she said, her eyes trying to adjust to the rampage of colors. "That's really . . . colorful!" She said it in a friendly way, trying not to discourage me. I put on a tank top, and we headed out to the town square.

There they were—my topless friends. All ten of them, and two queer boys from San Francisco in brightly colored wigs. The booby table was great. A big basket of the donuts, tons of female/queer/vegan-positive pamphlets, and fruits that resembled boobs in some way—grapes and such.

"Dexter?" Violet said between gritted teeth, motioning to my shirt. It was now or never, something like that, so I did it, I pulled my tank top off and felt the sun hit my skin like an albino rabbit's first exposure to daylight.

"Hi!" Everyone greeted me with warm, naked hugs, boobs mashing on my shooting stars, chipping the paint. Lilah smiled widely, handing me chalk and pointing out the "breast positive" drawings all over the town square.

"Hey will you please stop filming us?!" shouted a girl. I turned and there was Dick, with his camera out, yelling hoarsely that it was a "free country," and that if we were gonna be topless he had the right to film us. Dick was my friend Peyton's mom's boyfriend. My friends were arguing with him, their skin covered in queer nation stickers, reading stuff like "we dictate yer fashion" and "vagitarian dyke." Recognition hit Violet, and she whispered to me, "Oh my god, that's Dick!" Peyton hated him. He owned a very small black Chihuahua, and she hated the dog, too. I think Peyton thought of the dog as some sort of evil, screeching sidekick, because whenever Dick would yell at her the dog would yelp in unison at his side.

"Dick! Dick! I know you!" I walked toward him distracting the bad guy from my pals. He focused his camera on me as I walked up to him covering my chest with my arms. "I'm Peyton's friend. I'm her age."

"So what?" He growled, his little yippy dog yelping and jumping up like a grasshopper at his heels. "Please have respect and stop filming us," I concluded. It didn't faze him. A couple of girls started blocking his camera with their hands and he hit their arms away. Out of nowhere a police officer came to mediate. "What seems to be the problem, ladies?" He said it all Mr. Rogers-like, as if the bouncing bosoms and creepy guy filming them didn't give him a clue. It just goes to show that if you ignore something and play dumb it's like it's not really there.

We explained what was up. The officer turned to us real *slow*. "You have to know that if someone takes their shirt off—particularly ladies—they're gonna get attention. And this man can technically film you if yer in public."

We were so naïve. I mean, dealing with this kind of "attention" couldn't possibly have to do with why were marching!

"We have the right to be here and be safe!" said a topless bearded man in his forties, stepping in front of us as if it was his nubbins at stake. The three men stood there arguing, trying to decide the ladies' fate for us—big strong men who all knew best. For all the hubbub surrounding the men, it was as if we girls and our tits had been forgotten. Show stealers.

"But he's harassing us! And hit our arms." Lilah stepped in, curling her lip and running her hands through her short blond hair, all tuff and incredulous-like. Dick stood there, defending his right to push us around, pointing out that his camera was expensive.

"LEAVE THE GIRLS ALOOOONE!" bellowed the bearded hippy man, overshadowing our voices. The girls were angry, our faces tattered with the injustice, our big juicy fruits upright, pointed nipples ready to squirt intruding men in the eye with acid. I guess Dick realized that a bunch of sour-faced, screaming lesbos would not cut it for "girls gone wild" and he actually left. There were bigger problems at hand. What if the cop tried to shut us down? I was willing to get arrested; I believed in the cause, and would fight tooth and nail for it.

"Now, I'm gonna let you have the march—you seem like a nice respectful crowd," he paused, smirking at our low attendance. "As long as you guys don't cause any trouble, there's really no law that makes what yer doing illegal."

"Really, it's legal in Sebastopol?" Our group was dumbstruck. The officer had just negated any true need to have a march like this in the first place. Confused and relieved, we realized somehow the cop became our hero.

"I'll stand by in case anyone bothers you ladies."

That was good enough for us. Everyone rejoiced, the fillies were going to have their march! *It almost would have been better if he'd arrested us,* I thought. At least then we would have been fighting for something real, wouldn't have been patronized. What if this was an everyday occurrence, sitting outside family restaurants? Could the Sebastopol police continue to be so gracious? How long before the "law-abiding good girls" were handcuffed and hauled away, the injustice finally admitted?

I popped a donut in my mouth. I wasn't going to let it ruin my day.

The more I walked around—more than occasionally staring down at my shooting stars—the better I felt. It was time to rile up the crowd. I had been talked into being the MC, so I hopped onto the big concrete gazebo and grabbed the mic. Titty diva I was, I had the most festive rack there.

"Hi everyone! Welcome to BreastFest!" Twenty faces beamed up at me. "BABES's mission is to desexualize breasts! These laws are sexist! They are protecting the pornography industry, because you wouldn't have to buy pictures of tits if they were everywhere in society. We stand for women's liberation and the right to take yer shirt off on a hot day!" Twenty claps and cheers.

I felt fancy free, though my shorts were still hiked up awkwardly. I was a tuff feminist ring leader with my vegan friends now on stage with me, arms around each other, reciting the famous "Why I'm a Feminist" poem. But there was a stranger among us, a buxom topless women with a long purple and gray flowy skirt and long salt and pepper hair. She weaseled her way in between us, grabbing the microphone. She then told the crowd she was the leader of another jug-positive group named FREE TITTIES; in fact, the guy who hashed things out with the cop was her male lover. She talked endlessly, and then, to my horror, passed out tambourines and small drums. She'd also been circulating song lyric sheets. All I remember are the lines "The men like the titties! The babies like the titties, and like milk from the titties! The women like the titties . . ." and so on. She was like an overzealous parent, taking credit for her child's science project.

If you hadn't been handed an instrument then she linked your arms to someone else's, starting up a Do-Si-Do hoe-down, the chorus wringing in my ears, tambourines banging and rattling, images of milk and baby feeders overcoming me. All my friends looked as traumatized as I did. Violet snapped tons of pictures.

What could we do? We all started laughing hysterically, delving headfirst into the jamboree, immense approval showing on the Berkeley lady's face. She'd written the song herself and wanted to know if our groups could collaborate in the future.

There was a light breeze spreading over our goose-pimpled skin and jiggly boobs as we started marching. Signs in the air read, "I love my tits!" "Eliminate sexism!" "Desexualize breasts!" All twenty-something of us pressed onward, a small cluster screaming chants in a small town. The sun beat down on my bare skin, sweat fell down my back, and I was very much aware of being alive.

Colorful wigs bopped ahead of me. People in cars yelled, "Right on!" Random women joined us, flinging off their blouses. It was all so amazing. Some guys in an SUV snarled gross things at us, and some other guy told us we were traumatizing his son. For that afternoon we owned that town.

Heads high no matter what, breathless and enthusiastic, we walked all six blocks of my downtown, big fish revolutionaries.

Back at home I washed the acrylic paint off my melons, wincing at the pain emanating from them. They were burning spheres. It was incredible, my skin was completely red with sunburn except for distinct shooting stars, white and imprinted like a tattoo, staying like that for over a month.

A bra-burning "child of the goddess" once again.

A phoenix risen from the ashes.

The march was on the front page of the town paper.

I was there.

from:

nobody will find me here

by Katie Fricas

My favorite was the one where a bunch of B-list celebrities were forced to live together in a big mansion. They spent a lot of time invading the house's mini-fridge.

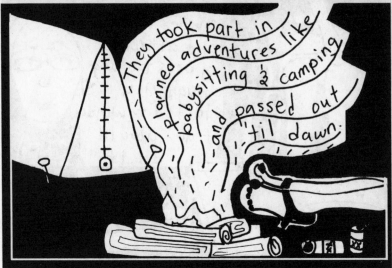

They took part in planned adventures like babysitting ½ camping and passed out 'til dawn.

To someone peering through our apartment window we might have appeared severely depressed
Were we really enjoying TV, or had entertainment gotten so bad that we could only find pleasure in watching things we actually hated?

Sunshine in the Fat End

Jenna Henry

Mama and Randy are fighting again. That sure ain't nothing new to me but it gets the neighbors here talking. Back before the hurricane, at our old park, the neighbors were used to Mama and Randy going round and round.

"Those two fight like cats and dogs," they'd say, and leave it at that. But here in the FEMA park people always yap about Mama and Randy and how that shit they're both on is gonna send 'em to Hell in a handbasket. Whatever that means. Seems to me if you go to Hell you don't go in anything. You just die and end up swimming in the lake of fire with the rest. That's what Pastor Roberts at First Baptist used to say Hell was anyway. A lake of fire full of all the bad folks in the world. Folks who didn't believe Jesus was the one who went and died for their sins on the cross way back when.

When I was little like JoJo, that used to scare me real good. I'd close my eyes so tight and pray to Jesus not to send me down to Hell. I begged Him to stay in my heart and never leave so that they'd let me into heaven when I died. I always felt like I had to ask Jesus to stay with me 'cause there were too many people who needed him and he might forget about me. Now I feel like I was sort of right because I don't pray much anymore. I bet Jesus has gone and forgot about me.

JoJo's sitting real close to me on the couch now and I didn't even notice he'd come 'cause he was so quiet about it. JoJo's real quiet all the time, though. He don't talk much on account of he's autistic. Mama used to get real jealous 'cause JoJo only talks to me when he ever does talk.

"I'm that boy's mama and you'd better not be tellin' him any different, Jessie. You hear me, girl?!" she'd say. She said things like that 'cause she had a lot of real mean boyfriends who didn't understand JoJo. They thought he was being smart 'cause he wouldn't answer when they called him, or he wouldn't mind what they said. JoJo'd get real upset and start wailing and crying and just throwing a big fit. I'd take him outside and set him down, talk to him.

"He ain't your real daddy, JoJo. Your real daddy ain't here, but if he was he'd fix mama's boyfriend real good." Mama would hear me sometimes, and so I guess she must have gotten scared that I was telling him she wasn't his real mama, too. I never did tell him that, though. She was just jealous.

JoJo still gets scared when Mama and Randy fight so he likes to stay close to me. I don't mind much. Only when I'm trying to watch something on TV and he wants me to play numbers with him. JoJo's real good with numbers. I think up the biggest numbers I can and he'll add 'em up quick.

"JoJo, what's 32,459 plus 95,682?" I ask him, and he don't take but a second or two to answer me.

"128,141." Only he says it a little different, like *hundrit twenny ay thousan hundrit forty one*. I understand him.

The door to the bedroom slams open and JoJo jumps. Mama comes out screaming something or other. I put my arm around JoJo and pull him tight to me. I can hear him breathin' real hard and so I try to distract him.

"JoJo, what's 542,390 plus 893,407?" He starts to answer me but then Mama stomps past us and he shuts up. When she moves through the living room I can smell that nasty smoke on her. She never used crack 'til she met Randy a few years ago. He's the one that got her on it. I don't remember exactly when it started. I just remember finding one of their pipes in the couch and me and JoJo were playing with it. I think we must have thought it was something to make music and we were trying real hard to figure out how to get it to play. Mama came in and saw us and snatched it real fast.

"This ain't no toy for kids, Jessie. This is a toy for grown-ups only. You ever see one of these again you leave it alone," she snapped.

"Yes ma'am," I said.

Seems like after that I started seeing the pipes a lot. Mama'd tell me to go get something out of her room for her and I'd see it lying on her dressing table next to her jewelry box. Or in the bathroom in the medicine cabinet. One time I found one under JoJo's bed and I threw it in the trash, but Randy found it and threw a big fit.

"Darla, what the hell's this doin' in the damned trash?!" he hollered.

"Shit, I don't fuckin' know!" she screamed back at him.

They got into a real big fight over that.

Randy stomps out of the bedroom now and the whole trailer shakes. It shakes even if he's not mad, though, 'cause he walks so heavy in those big boots he always wears. He's in the kitchen pulling drawers open and looking around inside of 'em, slamming 'em shut. Mama and him do that a lot. Always looking for something they never can find. Mama stomps past him and he catches her by her arm.

"Where do you think you're runnin' off to?" he says.

"I ain't stayin' here with you!" she screams and tries to get away.

"To hell you ain't. You get your ass back in there and find that fuckin' bag. It didn't just get up and walk away. I just bought if off Dylan after I got outta work and I know it ain't gone yet. Find it!" He shoves her off and she stumbles a little.

"Fuck you, Randy! I didn't fuckin' lose it! You probably shoved it up your ass for all I know!" she says.

Randy reaches back to hit her and I hold my hands over JoJo's eyes. He still hears it though and I feel him jump.

I know it's getting out of hand now so I grab JoJo by the hand and run him into our bedroom and slam the door. I open up our window and jump out onto the road. The white dust flies up all around me, and my feet crunch in the dirt. I turn back and JoJo's looking down at me.

"Come on, JoJo, jump. I'll catch you." He just stares back at me. We've done this before but sometimes he forgets what to do. "Come on, JoJo, I can't pick you up. Jump!" I tell him.

He stands there a little longer and then I see one of his legs come swinging out of the window. I grab his ankle to let him know I'll get him. His other leg comes out and I help him down the rest of the way. More dust flies up around us and we both cough. I grab his hand again and we walk down the road.

"You wanna go see Hank, JoJo? I bet he'll be real happy to see ya, huh? Ya'll two haven't hung around in a long time have ya? 'Bout a week it's been." I talk with JoJo as we walk through the trailers. He doesn't answer me, just squints in the sun. I know he hears me though.

Hank lives in trailer 63. When me and JoJo get close, his dog Mercedes comes running up to us. JoJo loves Mercedes. He gets a big grin on his face and goes to making all these sounds in the back of his throat when he sees him. Mercedes is a Doberman but she's a sweet girl, never hurt a fly. She licks JoJo's face and then walks alongside us 'til we get to the front door. Hank answers.

"Hey Jessie. Hey JoJo. Come on in," he says. Mercedes tries to follow us in but Hank shoves her back out. JoJo starts to whine and Hank sighs. "Oh alright, JoJo, but when Gloria gets home she's gotta go back out, ok?" he says, and lets Mercedes back in. JoJo pets Mercedes and they all sit down in the living room in front of the TV.

Hank is mostly JoJo's friend, but I knew him when we lived in the old park. We used to hang out in the woods by the park and hunt birds and squirrels and pretty much anything else we could find. Sometimes we'd hunt the cock-roaches in Hank's trailer if we were bored with birds and squirrels. We'd get Pringles chip cans and trap 'em inside and once we had a whole bunch we'd take 'em out back. We'd open up the can and spray the flame from a lighter with Aquanet and it was like a blowtorch. We'd light 'em all on fire. They'd make a whistling sound when they burned, and me and Hank would laugh and laugh. That was back when we was just kids and sorta liked the same kinda stuff. I'm almost sixteen now though and Hank's only eleven. JoJo's nine, so they get along better.

Gloria is Hank's older sister but she's more like his mama. Way back before the hurricane their mama ran off with some man she met at the bar where she worked and left them to fend for themselves. Lucky for Gloria she was almost eighteen anyway and had a job as a checker at the Piggly Wiggly. People used to ask where her mama went and she just told 'em she went on her honeymoon with her new hus-band. Sometimes she'd get mixed up if someone asked her twice 'bout where her mama went.

"Where'd you say she went on her honeymoon?"

And Gloria'd say, "Oh, they went to Bermuda."

"I thought you said it was Jamaica."

"No, Bermuda. They're down there on the beach drinkin' piña coladas and gettin' tans."

Hank told me that she just used the names from that Beach Boys song "Kokomo" to tell people where the "hon-eymoon" was at. After a few months people had it figured out that her mama wasn't coming back from wherever she went, so they stopped asking Gloria about it. I guess they felt sorry for her or something.

It ain't too long before Gloria shows up. She comes through the door in a real big hurry, carrying a bunch of groceries.

"Hank, I thought I told you about havin' Mercedes in the—oh hey there, JoJo! How are you doin', sugar?" Her voice changes when she sees him. Gloria just loves JoJo. JoJo turns and looks at Gloria, then looks back at the TV.

I come to Gloria's side to help her with the bags. "Here, let me take those for ya." I say, grabbing the heavy sacks from out of her arms.

"Oh Jessie, thanks a million, sugar," she says.

I like the way Gloria calls me *sugar*. It gives me a funny feeling in my stomach. Kinda like when you're on one of them great big roller coasters at the Fair right before it's about to drop down into a big dip.

Gloria goes over to JoJo and wraps her arms around him. She kisses his cheek and messes his hair. "How are you, darlin'? Huh? You doin' ok?" she says softly. JoJo puts his hand up on her arm and leaves it there for a minute. Gloria kisses it and then moves over to Hank. "How are you doin', honey?" she asks him. "I'm ok." He says. "Anyone stop by?" she asks. "Nope. Just JoJo and Jessie," he answers, never taking his eyes off the TV. Gloria kisses him and walks back to the door.

She heads outside and I follow. I help her get the rest of the sacks out of the trunk of her beat-up Monte Carlo. One of her neighbors from back at the old park was a mechanic, and he sold it to her real cheap when he found out she was on her own with Hank. "It ain't much to look at, darlin', but it's a good runner. I know 'cause I worked on it myself," Bill told her. And he was right. The old heap had lasted her this long with hardly any trouble. Gloria says it's 'cause she talks to it. "A car just needs a little love like anything else," she says, rubbing the dusty dashboard. "Don't you, honey? You just need to know you're appreciated."

While we're bent over the trunk getting the groceries Gloria turns to me. "You alright, sugar? Is your mama fightin' with Randy again?" she asks.

"What makes you say that, huh?" I smile.

"Well there ain't no use in you tryin' to fib to me 'cause it's all over your face," she says, and slams the trunk shut. "That pretty smile of yours ain't foolin' me one bit." She heads back inside and I follow her again.

She's already putting stuff away when I get in and kick the door shut behind me. I watch as she flies through each bag, almost like she's dancing she moves so quick through everything. All the while she's asking me questions in a sorta code so that Hank and JoJo don't make out what she's saying. "Were they doin' that thing again?" she says.

"Yep," I answer.

"Anything else go down?"

"Yep."

"Oh Lord." She shoves five or six boxes of macaroni and cheese into a cabinet and slams it shut. "Well you and JoJo can just stay here with me and Hank tonight, ok? Don't you worry about a thing. I'll make us up some Hamburger Helper and we'll watch a video or somethin'."

"Ok," I tell her. She pulls a glass down from another cabinet, pours some tea, and stands there at the counter drinking it.

"Mmm! I was so thirsty," she sighs, and then stops herself. "Look at me. I must be the rudest person in the whole wide world. You'd think I wasn't raised with any manners at all! You want some tea?" she asks.

"Sure, I guess I am a little thirsty," I say. "It's the heat! It's always like an oven outside here. But I suppose I got the government to thank for my electric bill. Ain't like they put up any nice shade trees around to cool things off a little bit," she says. Gloria and probably everyone else at the FEMA park complain about their air conditioning bill. Gloria's is almost always about to get shut off 'cause it gets so high and most of the time she don't make that much money up at the IHOP where she works now. She tried to keep fans blowing in the windows instead but it didn't do much for the bill, so she kept the air conditioner on again.

Gloria brings me the tea in a glass with orange and lemon slices printed all over it. I take a drink and close my eyes. She makes the best sweet tea I have ever had, hands down. "Secret's in the sugar," she says. I don't know what it is she uses, all's I know is I love it. She sits down across from me at her little dinette and we sip our tea and watch Hank and JoJo playing Sega Genesis. "Boy, JoJo sure loves to watch Hank play, huh?" Gloria says.

"Yeah he does. He don't really understand about how to work the controller or anything, but he likes to watch," I say.

"That's the best thing I found at the thrift store yet, that Sega Genesis. I wish I could afford to get him one of them newer games they got out now. That Playstation 2 or whatever that thing is. Nintendo somethin' or other. I just ain't got the money for it," she says, and I nod. Then after a minute or two she leans across the dinette and lowers her voice just a hair above a whisper. "See, that's what I want Hank to think, Jessie. But I'm really savin' up for one of them Playstations. His birthday is just a few weeks away and I'm gonna get him one. But you can't say anything. It's gotta be kept secret. I want it to be a big surprise," she says.

"Oh, I won't tell nobody, Gloria. Not a soul." Her eyes get all big and she puts a finger across her lips. I nod and she smiles real wide. She must have the most beautiful smile out of any girl I've seen. Her teeth are just perfect. And she never had no braces or nothing when she was a kid.

We sit for a little while longer not saying much of nothing, and then Gloria jumps up like she was in a trance or something. "That dinner ain't gonna make itself now is it!" She starts browning the hamburger in her great big frying pan and the smell makes my mouth just water. I ain't had nothing to eat since lunch at school 'cause Mama and Randy don't keep much of anything in the kitchen. Most of what I can scrounge up I give to JoJo. I've made him all kinda strange meals before. Saltine crackers crunched up into tomato paste, macaroni with a little bit of ranch dressing, mayonnaise sandwiches, cheerios with chicken broth. I have to beg him to eat sometimes.

"I know it ain't McDonald's, JoJo, but you gotta eat 'cause it's all I can find. Please, JoJo? Come on, just try a little for me." Sometimes he'd go to crying and Mama or Randy'd get upset.

"What's wrong with him?" Mama'd ask.

"He's hungry," I'd tell her.

"Well how come you didn't get him somethin' to eat?" she'd say.

"Ain't hardly anything to eat. He don't want what I made him." Then Randy'd stick his big nose into things and yell at JoJo.

"You quit that cryin', boy, and eat what Jessie made you. Keep that shit up and I'll give you somethin' to really cry about." Lot of nights he'd just cry himself out and finally go to sleep.

I set the table real nice for Gloria. Fold the paper towels into little triangles and everything. "Well now I didn't realize this was such a classy dinner we was havin'," Gloria says. "I should have dressed for the occasion." She goes running off into her bedroom and comes back out in a dress with great big sunflowers all over it.

"What'd you go and do that for?" I ask, smiling at her.

"Well I couldn't dine in my dirty old work uniform now could I?" she says. "You look real nice," I tell her. She smiles and grabs the pan off the stove. "Come on boys, soup's on!"

She starts spooning out big helpings of the Hamburger Helper. Hank and JoJo come sit down and JoJo starts shoveling his in so fast he starts choking 'til his eyes go to watering. Hank hits him on the back a couple of times. "Oh sweetie, if I'da known you was so hungry I'd given you a little snack or somethin'," Gloria says, and looks at me real concerned like. I'm trying not to do the same thing JoJo did myself, but it's real hard. I'm barely chewing at all before

I got the next forkful ready. I see Hank raising his eyebrows, looking at me and then at Gloria, and I feel my face going red and hot. I slow down a little, but I'm still real embarrassed. And being embarrassed in front of Gloria's about the worst feeling in the world. Makes me wanna just disappear.

But then Gloria makes me feel a little better. "Boy, I never felt so proud of my Hamburger Helper in all my life. Sure you ain't just tryin' to flatter me?" she says.

"It's real good, Gloria. Thank you." I smile.

"I'll have to have you and JoJo come over all the time and I'll start feelin' like that one chef they got on the TV. What's his name? Kinda heavy-set guy. Looks like he might be Italian or somethin'. Always hollerin' when he cooks," she says.

"BAM!" Hank says.

"Yea, that's what he says! What's his name, Hank?"

"Emeril," Hank answers.

"Emeril! I'll be just like Emeril right here in trailer 63. And they're just gonna have to find a way to fit all them big cameras in my kitchen."

"Well I bet folks would like lookin' at you a lot more than that Emeril," I tell her. "Ya think so?" she says, and pulls her long red hair up. She bats her eyes and puckers up her lips and we both start laughing.

After supper I clear the table and wash up and Gloria picks out a video for all of us to watch. Her and Hank argue back and forth for a little bit between *Terminator 2* and *Batman* before making their minds up on *Batman*. I am real glad they decided on it 'cause that Arnold Schwarzenegger is just awful. I don't know where he learned to act from, but seems to me if it was a school they should just go on ahead and shut it down.

JoJo and Hank fall asleep with Mercedes not too far along into it, so it's just me and Gloria. The Joker's throwing all that money off his big parade float. It's flying through the air like leaves. "What would you do with all that money, Gloria?" She laughs.

"Oh, I'll tell you what I'd do," she says, turning toward me. "I'd buy a great big old house somewhere far, like California or Hawaii. I'd put the most beautiful things inside. All that newfangled fancy stuff you see on the TV in famous people's houses. Know what I'm talkin' about? Those nice chandeliers and pretty rugs and leather sofas. Then I'd get me one of them cute little dogs like that Britney Spears has and carry it around with me everywhere." I shake my head, laughing.

"What about you, Jessie? What would you do with a big pile of money?" she asks.

"Oh wow, I don't even know," I tell her.

"Well you gotta know!" She grins real big and I start to think on it for a little bit. She's watching me real close, waiting to hear what I'm gonna say, like I'm about to tell her my biggest secret. "Well . . . ," I start to say, but I don't get to go on 'cause there's a knock on the door. For a minute, my stomach gets all twisted up inside 'cause I'm thinking it might be Mama or Randy come to tell us to get home. I don't wanna go home, though. When I'm at Gloria and Hank's, I don't ever wanna go.

It ain't them, though. I know it soon as I hear Gloria say, "Well hey you." She steps back and T. J. comes in looking tired.

"Hey, how ya' doin'?" He pulls her close and starts to kiss her and I look back to the TV. All the folks in Gotham City are choking to death right there in the street. The Joker's laughing at 'em all.

"Hey Jessie, how are ya', girl? I ain't seen you in a while." T. J. sits down on the couch next to me.

"I'm alright, T. J.," I say, but it's a lie. I wish he hadn't come over 'cause I was having a real nice time with Gloria by myself. That's always the trouble with most men. They show up and interrupt things, make it all weird-like. I suppose T. J. ain't so bad; he don't treat Gloria bad or nothing. He don't beat up on her or call her names like Randy does to Mama. But I wish he hadn't come over just the same.

"What are ya'll watchin'?" T. J. asks.

"*Batman*," Gloria says.

"This the very first one?" he asks. "Yea," I tell him.

"Aw, come on. You seen this a bunch of times, Gloria. Let's go to bed, I'm tired," he says.

"But I'm watchin' it with Jessie."

"I'm sure she'll be fine without ya. Come on, honey." He gets up and starts walking to the bedroom, but stops behind the chair where Gloria's sitting and starts kissing on her neck. She goes to giggling and squirming around.

"Stop it, T. J.!" she says, all playful like. He goes into the bedroom. "Let me get you a blanket, Jessie." She goes away and comes back with the yellow blanket I always use when

I'm here, and a pillow. "You need to borrow some of my clothes for school in the morning, sugar?" she asks.

"Naw, I'm ok. I'll just go change at my house a little early," I tell her.

"You wanna go sleep in Hank's bed since he's out here?"

"No, that's ok. JoJo might wake up and get scared if I ain't where he can see me right away."

"Alright, well sleep good. I'll see you in the mornin'. I got a double to work tomorrow so I'll be up real early." She gives me a hug and I can smell her perfume on me even after she's left.

It ain't too long before I'm laying there on the couch listening to Gloria and T. J. going at it. I can hear the headboard hitting the wall and the water from their waterbed sloshing around. I feel things while I'm listening to 'em that I can't seem to figure out. I feel real mad in the first place for some reason. Not so much at Gloria, mostly T. J. I feel my blood just start rushing up to my face when I hear him moaning and groaning. Makes me just wanna go in there and pull him right off of Gloria and push him out the door butt naked. But when I'm listening to Gloria it's not the same. I get that funny feeling in my stomach like when she calls me sugar, except it's stronger. My heart starts beating real fast and my mouth goes dry. I feel like I wish I was in that bed with her, making her breathe all heavy. I listen to T. J. talking and I close my eyes. I imagine that it's me and not him. "That's it baby, you're doin' fine. You're doin' just fine," I whisper.

In the Parlor

Tamara Llosa-Sandor

They viewed grandma at this funeral home right on the main drag in pittsburg, where railroad avenue crossed with highway 4 and led past the fast-food stops, gas stations, and mini strip-malls. the home sat sandwiched between a wells fargo bank and walgreens: a squat stucco building with a shingled, tar-colored roof and a sprawling parking lot glinting with pebbles of broken beer bottles. inside, the carpet was a forest green, the walls varying shades of purple with textured stripes. the double doors opened to a long wide room with cheap ornate chairs set up in a grid. the ceiling was low and seemed to press down on us as we squeezed into the parlor.

i sat front row to my dead grandmother, thinking about how all these old filipinos who came to say the rosary would soon die, how the ones who didn't come were either dead or dying. i thought about my mother, sitting one row back. how she would probably get diabetes, too, a side result from a life full of fast food and impulse shopping. it would be an american achievement to die saddled with credit card debt, a closet full of beanie babies, and swatch watches; her kitchen overstuffed and unusable, a stack of wonder bread bags on the counter and kraft slices in the fridge; the collection of special edition wheaties boxes toppling out of the pantry; all the years of drive-thrus at mcdonald's, burger king, wendy's, in-and-out, church's chicken; all the craving stops at the donut shop next to safeway or at nation's for a coconut cream pie; all the trips to toys "r" us, target, and costco.

they viewed grandma in a funeral home right on the main drag in pittsburg. the street traffic made the room vibrate and grandma's face jiggle. she lay tucked into a shiny white dress i'd found in her closet, hands folded just-so over a black purse. i remembered the dress from a set of photographs i came across while sifting through the dated treasures in her dresser drawers. the photographs were in an old kodak envelope that'd gone all stained and brittle, the 3x5s themselves with a liquid dust stickiness across their gloss and thumbprints marking the corners. the prints showed an event, the dress-up kind, outside in the sun. the hairstyles bigger, clothes slimmer, colors more earthy. then grandma in her department store white dress, posing with someone over a foldout table with a plentiful filipino spread. grandma loved food: cooking, eating, feeding family, friends, guests, packing tupperware to go. now she lay in her dress, split down the back to fit over her chubby body.

auntie ludie sat next to me, whispering a prayer to herself. she placed the ball of crumpled tissues she'd been holding onto her lap and reached under her chair for her purse, one of

thing upside down. giggling when her stockpiled catholic saint cards came spilling out like a winning poker hand.

in all the purses, grandma kept a two-dollar bill, folded haphazardly then tucked neat into a small ziplock baggie and slipped into a safe zippered flap. my mother explained that this was for good luck, this special money that was kept inside, never to be spent.

my grandparents came here because america was the better place to go. better than the philippines or okinawa or guam. better than manila's sweltering humidity, its eight-hour traffic, its roaming scraggly dogs. california was better than arizona or nevada or utah. the neighborhood in pittsburg better than an always-revolving army base. a shared yard better than none. a house with a concrete patio better than the recycled military unit. the railroad two blocks away better than booming supply trucks and air force planes overhead.

in 1964 grandma said here. they would stop here. she would make angel food cake and trade it with neighbors for homemade enchiladas and fresh-caught fish from the sacramento river. she'd gossip on the porch with the other filipino wives while their husbands finished their service. when the men returned on leave, they'd bring home stacks of square photographs from london, germany, hong kong, hawaii, and everybody would gather around to see where they had been.

here, the girls walked to school and grandma ran errands with friends until grocery bags filled the backseat and trunk. in the afternoon the kids played in the street and put pennies on the railroad tracks, comparing whose flattened copper looked the weirdest. here, you could find work if you wanted it, piling in a car pool of girlfriends in the pre-dawn to sort through chocolates at sees or cans at hunt's tomato. things in california were easier and the things that weren't easy like being called a chink or jap or gook, like someone asking if you ate your dog, like kids pulling their eyes back to make them slanty, like late-night phone callers with twangy central valley voices telling you to go back to whichever foreign fucking place you came from—well, the things that weren't easy, that's what the other filipinos were for: they could nod and hum in agreement, sitting on the porch or stirring something the kitchen. it was worth it to be here.

grandma was an optimist. if someone said something disagreeable, she'd make a face like she'd just swallowed the sinagang lemon juice and say no no no. they had moved from the philippines. relatives still there sat in the humidity and sweated out the jealousy, then made plans to move here. for those who couldn't come over, regardless of sweating and planning, grandma sent back money. she called them with bargain international calling cards grandpa bought her each week at the philipino store. his errands always capped off at ace hardware to get a lottery ticket. grandma wrote long letters to manila, to her closest brother and sister, to her distant siblings. she wrote to friends, cousins, aunties, and uncles. she wrote to her mother and father and his ex-wives. she wrote on onion skin sheets in a fluid, well-studied cursive, with the date and place noted at the top, and always, the name of god invoked at the bottom. the letters were full of formal news, like how the kids were doing in school, like who had come over to visit some afternoon and what dishes she had cooked for them. for grandma, everyone was too skinny. and why, when safeway or save-mart was so plentiful? eat eat she'd say to anyone who walked into the house, pointing them toward the kitchen. she would pack up big balikbayan boxes to send back. the heavy-duty cardboard boxes stuffed with things that my mom and auntie had grown out of: barbies and lincoln logs, rain boots and sunday dresses. grandma packed tooth-paste, towels, sugar, soap, whatever she could fill up on at a two-for-one or buy-three-get-one-free or blue-light special or in bulk at the flea market.

unlike most other filipinos who'd come over, my grand-parents never went back, not even to visit. if i asked my mother why, she'd say that grandpa had a bad knee, that he couldn't sit for the eighteen-hour flight. she'd say grandma suffered from such nausea and illness on the way here, she swore never to repeat the trip. if i asked my mother if she ever wanted to go back, she'd say, why would i want to go there?, twisting "there" like the knob of a door she had shut. if she caught me in the midst of asking grandma why, she'd hssst, make her eyes wide and shake her head at me and i would reel my question back in and close my mouth over it. one time i tried a different angle. i said i would like to go back, to see manila, to visit relatives. oh mah-gaud grandma said, putting both hands over her stomach and bending into them like she hurt there, her face scrunched up with the sinagang lemon juice. no no boji, aye! what is there for you? you stay here and make good grades for grandma.

this was the official story posted and nailed to the door my mother kept a handle on. they had traveled east to the states, then west, settling in california, the very heart of the gold mountain. it hardly mattered that it was a cliché or that the gold gleamed brightest in the checkout line. they set up lawn chairs in the front yard of their promised land and plopped me in the center of the kiddie pool. they were here.

But what was back there that made grandma's face sour? what was their life like before? in the philippines? in the military? my questions gathered quietly while grandma laid down a crisp bill for every *a* on my report card.

I was the first to be born here and that meant keeping my eyes forward and feet moving. the fledgling step into my inheritance of opportunity happened in the backyard of my grandparents' house. my diapered butt seated on a cool concrete slab tall enough to see over the fence into the pasture that lay between the neighborhood and the pg&e plant. grandma was hanging the laundry that she had most likely used two kinds of detergent and a fabric softener on while grandpa barbecued spareribs. i pointed at the cows grazing on the california golden summer grasses, shook my bottle, and said bahbah cow.

milk, by the quart, the carton. the honey was in the sweetness. my mouth was open but it wasn't slung back, aching. i wasn't choking on dust kicked up by wagon wheels or the sagging tires of jalopies. i arrived after they had inhaled the airplane exhaust. my grandparents hit it pretty good for immigrants. there were always two jugs of milk in the fridge, in case one ran out. pointing at the cows in the pasture, i shook my empty bottle and grandma refilled it.

Coming-Out versus Sex versus Making Love

Meliza Bañales

Coming-out young was different. There were stages to coming-out, a system of revealing. You had to pick and choose just the right moment to tell various facts to various people. I would tell my mom about Ana, how I liked her, and she would cringe—not from disgust but from fear, the fear of what might happen to me if this information fell into the wrong hands. I wouldn't tell my friends, though. I wasn't dangerous enough. And even though it was the early nineties I was still in South Central LA where there was no PFLAG to save me.

Ana was a world of frustration. I made her that way. When she and her mother moved to Hollywood she made lots of gay boy-friends, went to Fairfax High, drank lattés, and shopped at bookstores. She was immersed in gayness and I was stuck in the other side of the ghetto with Pioneer Chicken and Pick'n Save. She encouraged my escapes, my running away to her empty apartment on Friday afternoons to lie on her bed, smoking cigarettes, and kissing my breasts.

She loved to be naked as much as I did and we would revel in our nudity, feeling adult and strikingly sexual. Then, at night, we would meet up with her gay boy-friends—beautiful Latino rebels with dark jeans, biker boots, James Dean jackets, and Morrissey pompadours—to go to The Arena, the all-ages queer dance club. We would dress in short-shorts and tall boots wearing lipstick and mascara and she would hold me from behind in line, trailing her mouth against the back of my neck. She had found a community, a gay culture she could relate to and be familiar with. She was so casual in her affection toward me in these moments, as if the whole world had always been gay, always seen two girls swallow each other in hands and kisses.

But I ran away too often to her. She wanted to escape too. Wanted to feel like she had a place to go that didn't involve her mother, her empty room, and neon signs. I hated her coming to my house, doing things with my friends. My friends were all girls, straight girls who fucked guys for pleasure and talked about hair and clothes. Ana was used to her boys' town, running with the pretty boys and their Smiths CDs and Bukowski novels. My friends could not care less about Bukowski, and House music was the only decent sound to blast from your bedroom window. And Ana was a secret in this part of the city. She was my "friend" from Fairfax, the friend who came over once in a while and spent the night in my twin bed, the way all girls spent the night with each other growing up.

"When are you gonna tell them about me? About us?" she would ask over the phone after her visits. I would sit there in my room, panting like a wounded animal into the receiver trying to make my brain work, to come up with an excuse, something to appease her for a little while since I didn't have a real answer.

"Look, it's just gonna take time."

"It's been eight months, Meliza. I don't know what you're waiting for."

And she would take a deep breath and then exhale heavily. Then I would say I had to go and hang up the phone so quickly that our conversation fell to the floor, a small dusty mess that I would grind into the carpet.

Then there was sex and intimacy. It was not Sex we were having, Ana would tell me, but Making Love. We both had lost our virginity to boys, she at fifteen and myself at sixteen—and we decided that was Sex. Sex was easy and quick and something you did so you could get it over with and move on. It was an automatic act, something that took little effort, especially with high-school boys. It was as routine as eating and combing your hair or washing towels: a chore, one that kept you busy but proved to be as exciting as a rainy day.

Making Love took time. It was a process of being careful, of hitting all the right spots with intention and precision, like playing the piano or tuning a guitar. It required Ana and I to look at each other in the daylight or morning, sun bleeding through the blinds and falling on the sheets like zebra stripes. It was required patience and could not be rushed. Ana would climb on top of me, her brown hair falling over me, hunched over like a cat on a fence, moving up and down, kissing me all over. Making me quake and moan, making me sexy and safe. Sometimes she would stay up there for almost forty-five minutes, just kissing me and grazing my skin with her nipples. I couldn't help but slip two fingers into her, easily going in and out, my other hand cupping her ass in a gentle, vanilla rocking while she called me "Mija" and "Baby," cumming all over my stomach in smooth breaths. We would Make Love at all hours of the day, falling asleep, waking up, smoking, and laughing.

But we never went down on each other. Exploring her cunt with my mouth would ruin our Love Making, I was convinced. I was afraid of her cunt, afraid that going down on her would fuck up the Love Making. I knew once I came face-to-face with her cunt she would find out what a big amateur I was and then everything between us would become Sex, tired and dismal. Though she desperately wanted to plunge her face between my legs, and though I really wanted her to, I would stop her, steer her away to my thigh or back up to my mouth where I knew how to work it, the machinery. Having her go down on me would mean I would have to go down on her—it was only fair, I thought, like an eye for an eye, a fair exchange of pleasure. Once it was my turn I wouldn't know what to do with her. I couldn't deal with her disappointment. Instead I would masturbate for her, massaging my clit with my index finger and ejaculate onto her sheets and she'd stroke my head and tell me how beautiful I was and how good I smelled; that she wouldn't wash her sheets for a few days so she could continue to get wet off the scent of me.

Though she was patient and never pushy about the oral sex issue, I always walked away ashamed, feeling like a punk, like I had chickened out. I felt inadequate, and for a second I identified with the plight of horny high school boys who went out with cute girls and just couldn't get it up. I was a limp dick, a dyke who couldn't do her job. Ana, however, didn't seem to notice. She would spoon me from behind and tell me how lucky she felt to be with me, that we were lucky that *La Vírgen* made us *Lesbiana*—and best of all Femmes—and that amidst all the smog and noise we were able to find each other and know what to do in our nakedness. Weren't we lucky to know all that, she'd ask.

After a year and two months Ana and I split up. I knew it was my fault. I couldn't come all the way out with her and I was a limp dick, a dyke who couldn't go down and take care of business. Ana never said those things. But I felt them and I was at an age where all of my life was based on feelings and instinct. We decided to stay friends.

She started to go out more and more. Hollywood was different from South Central that way. All those lights and strips of clubs and bars and attractive people doing what they wanted—it was all too tempting and only a matter of time before she fell into it. She got pregnant from a one-night stand and her mother said it was time to leave. The party was over. They were going to move to Texas where the days were slower and the sun slapped you into shape.

Ana told me getting pregnant was a direct consequence of

Sex. Making Love had consequences, too, but not physical ones. It was only your heart that got hurt. Sex's consequences involved huge life changes like babies, and having to buy new clothes, and moving and not allowing yourself to dream anymore. Sex was ruthless and unfair because it wasn't based in anything real. It was an act, one that often happened when drugs and alcohol occupied the mind and the body was left to fend for itself.

Ana moving away marked the ultimate sadness in my life. She sent me letters for a couple of years after that, even when I was in college. I saw her one more time, when I was twenty-one and visiting my parents in LA. She called me, having remembered my old phone number after so many years and I met her for a drink on Santa Monica Boulevard. Then we went to a motel where we didn't have to give our names and we Made Love in loud, tender fury. The next day we had pancakes at IHOP and then she got on a plane to Arizona and I would never see or hear from her again.

Except once. My mother told me a woman had called the house and when my mother answered the phone, the voice on the other line whispered, "Míja, is that you?" When my mother asked who was calling, the caller hung up. Maybe it was Ana, I thought, maybe she's in trouble. Or maybe it was a wrong number. There were so many Míjas in the world, especially in LA, all receiving whispers and phone calls in the dark to numbers so old phonebooks no longer carried them anymore. It was memory that allowed the numbers to appear, like smoke in a sunset over Redondo Beach or a neighbor's dripping faucet.

The Part about the Pigeons

Jess Arndt

Day 1: Two pigeons arrived today on my stoop and have nestled themselves under the ladder up to the roof. As if there aren't enough pigeons scrounging rough and ready on Mission Street—fat hustlers waiting for a deal. Now I have two of my very own, and like unwanted houseguests, they have dropped haunch and seem entirely convinced to stay. Whenever I open my window they half-waddle, half-fly themselves into a frenzy of feathers. I think it's a guilt thing. They want me to feel the dark, head-hanging shame of having inconvenienced them.

Day 2: I slept for shit last night, tossing and turning all over my room. Every time I drifted off, their cooing swelled into a crescendo of sound. The buttery, plump, insistent noise of two birds purring to each other no more than three feet from my head. I opened my window and sent them loud and heavy into the night. But soon they were back with a thud, thud, and the cooing started up again. Opera singers with chocolate pudding stuck in their throats.

Day 3: They are here for good. When I walked up the stairs and into my room this afternoon, the thick, mildly fishy smell of pigeon was ripe in the air. They have staked out their claim. I am to be hunted by pigeons. Even worse, the cooing has escalated into rampant pigeon sex sounds, complete with grunting, squeaking, and erratic wing beats. Here we are and all around us the world is breaking itself down like a digestive tract with too much juice and then there are these pigeons. I stare out my window, silently begging them to fight.

Day 4: This morning my car was covered in a thick coat of pigeon shit. I would like very much to believe that it is from the gruff pigeons that hang out on the corner of Capp Street, tugging ratty pieces of wire and broken glass around in their beaks. My birds are just too busy doing it and cooing to drop such a load of waste. Still, I glare at them tonight before going out. It's pretty ballsy that in this life—where no one is really happy with anyone else anymore—two pigeons get to sit pretty, making hay and home. Aren't they supposed to be out ratting around or flying or something?

Day 5: I got back from work last night shoved up to the gills in whiskey. When I opened my window to smoke one last cigarette against the dark spilly night, the pigeons shoved off as usual. Then I noticed it. Way back in the corner, down where the wood and tar paper meet, is a little white and brown speckled egg. All oval and perfect and bare. I shut my window quick so they could get back to the business of keeping it warm. It was April cold out without any fog.

Day 6: Where is their nest? All I can see of it are four or five skinny pieces of grass and string lying next to the egg. What poor planning. I have stopped opening my window altogether, but still they are only on their egg about half of the time. Out on Mission, hundreds of other pigeons hustle dopey and brave between the buses and bike tires, picking at taco beans and cigarette butts. I drop an old wool hat out the window for them to use in what appear to be emergency conditions, but they refuse to touch it.

Day 7: It is hard for me to be in my room at all. The egg just sits there, un-nested. We don't have the right kind of sun to keep it warm. There is nothing tropical in the San Francisco wind. The pigeons have stopped cooing and instead seem to be muttering to each other under their breath. I think the egg will die. And what am I doing, thinking like this about one pigeon, more or less. Still they are working at the egg in their pigeon-toed roundabout kind of way, while it sits in the corner, lamely. I leave my room to stop worrying about it and then every roly-poly pigeon reminds me of the little awkward family on my roof. Who's ever seen a baby pigeon anyway?

Day 8: The pressure is too much. I have started pretending that they are stray parrots carousing from some place far out of reach. Shuffling tired from the drunk rip of sea air. Throats full of curses and stained maps. Just stopping momentarily at my window to rascal a bit and then out again. Out and over into another bawdy night. But when I wake up tomorrow morning, they will still be there, pigeons, sitting on a bum nest. Who needs it? It makes you sad.

Day 9: It is raining today in that weepy smear kind of way that acts like it will never stop. I look out my window past the rough sketch of their nest and up toward the bald crown of Bernal Hill, all brown and slashy with rain. Three telephone poles spike from it, crooked in my view, like a tri-masted ship sailing crippled from storm. I picture cannons and squawking and sailors with knives. The poles break gravity. How their earthquaked stance is ever dodgy, and yet somehow they hold static, teetering tottering, but never diving down. My eyes drift to the nest, expecting to find it sodden and dull. But by some trick the catapult tilt of my eaves have blocked the rain almost entirely. The way the swollen wood soldiers up to the sky. Leaving my pigeon sitting calmly, almost queenlike, in between the drips and drops.

Boots for Tula

Rhiannon Argo

Her new boss had told her, *something short and sweet*. A good stripper girl name, but all names other girls had used before. Where were those girls now?

"I'd call you whatever you wanted me to," I tell her as the T-shirt carousel spins circles around and around. One hundred white medium-sized T-shirts to be screen-printed by dawn with the emblem of some karate school. We both pull the squeegee at once, slide then scrape. She refills my cup with vodka and cranberry juice. Drunk, the lines never come out straight. Drunk, the paint spatters all over and smears our skin. Drunk, her pink-lipped smile is so distracting. Pitter-patter over two lips. Pitter-patter up the stairs. Upstairs through the wood slats of the floor, the place we crash, where the guys party into the late-late night and then pass out. Pitter-patter past Baby Blue and he still has more drugs.

"You girls almost done down there?"

"Yeah." Pull down. Slide then spin. "Seventy-one. Seventy-two."

"Fuck, mine's crooked." Our pile of mess-ups in the corner keeps growing. Slide then spin around again.

"Roxy," she says. "Coco," she says. I tell her that I heard once that your stripper name is your first dog's name paired with the first street you ever lived on. "Princess, was my dog's name and we first lived on Tulips Court, *Princess Tulips*," she laughs, "Then what's yours?"

"I never had a dog and we moved so much to remember streets," I say.

"That's why you're not gonna be the stripper," she says. "It's fate." Around again and then scrape back and forth.

Another smoke break and we pull open the wide garage door and look out at barren city buildings that slant back from the shop. She picks the dried paint off her thumbnail. "I'm not gonna be some plain Jane anymore," she says. Drunk, she pulls me over and does a shimmy-shimmy. Drunk, my tongue slips in her mouth and she laughs it back out.

"Seventy-three, seventy-four." A purple haze is creeping up over the tops of the buildings and thawing out the edges of the night sky. "Shit, there's no way we're gonna have 'em all done by morning, we better throw in the mess-ups."

"Seventy-five, seventy-six."

"Tula," she decides, and by that time the sun is glaring through the windows and squinting into our tired eyes.

There's the sound of a beer can being popped open and that's all I can hear for a few seconds. The echo of it in my ears, everything else goes silent, like when the boys put on porn and it's in the background on mute while they party all night. This is what the crowded living room feels like. I can't hear Tula telling some story, I can just see her mouth flip-flopping around like a slippery little red fish and I can't hear the guys all around her, the always different but still all the same to me guys—skate shoes and tattooed forearms, sly grins and hands that hold pipes, beer cans, and baggies.

I have a few places that I go to in this house. Late at night it's the bathroom with the cool side of the tub against my back and a door that locks. The other place is a slanted room of a closet near the front door. I can even sleep in there if it comes to that—thing is it's not so good after dark because all you got is the crack of light that comes under the door. I need light to draw in the sketchbook I keep tucked away in a dusty corner.

But tonight the places that I go in this house aren't far away enough. I want my board but it got run over, drunk and stupid, shooting down the hill like we do to go to the Mission bars. It flew right out from under my feet and was snapped in two by the cars zooming up Fell Street. When the guys are around there's always a row of boards in the hallway, the dingy white wall has a permanent smudgy streak of skate wheel dust. I run my hands over the tops of the decks as I head for the door, grab the narrowest deck, and I'm gone, the cool mist hitting my face as the board slaps down on concrete.

I drag one foot all the way down the hill and the rubber heats up against the sidewalk, so close to my skin I can feel the potential sting. A night like this and I want to fall, hit the street like a smashed bottle. I want to fall because I think maybe then I will cry, sprawled out on the lonely street I will look at my bloody palms and then look around and see how completely alone I am and then the tears will come. Yeah, but it never happens that way.

I'm not far enough away till I've been skating around for hours and the night fog gots me pulling my hoody-hood up tight over my ears. I know I'm by the Opera House by the way the sidewalk sparkles up shimmery beneath the street grime. I love the angles of this city, how movement comes from all sides and keeps my body ready for each sharp swerve of the board. I cut across an orange glowing bus that looks like a floating spaceship creeping through the gray-gray, and I roll past the flickering fluorescent glow of the twenty-four-hour donut shop, its sweet crusty, sugary smells lingering in the air. I stop at the donut shop, duck into the bathroom, and rummage through my backpack for the beer I took from the house.

There's this flyer in my bag for a girl party tonight; I picked it up earlier today from a counter covered with colorful flyers at the vintage store where me and Tula sell our old clothes. We had lugged two whole garbage bags of stuff onto the bus and up the hill to the Haight. It was our last draw stuff since we hadn't gone back home for "shopping" trips lately.

When we first moved to the city the only way we got cash was by stealing clothes from the malls in our sub-urban town and then reselling them at the vintage stores. We started making a little cash helping Baby Blue with his screen-printing business, but the clothes swindle was the best deal. We once got cut a check for almost two hundred bucks. That was back when our friend Lacey worked at this major department store and tipped us off that the sensor system was temporarily out of commission. That was a real rush, walking through those wide doors with bags full of clothes with the sensors still on and praying that Lacey wasn't bullshitting. Also how relaxing it was to be able to pop sensors off at our own leisure, sitting on my bed surrounded by piles of clothes and taking care not to fuck up the fabrics while perfecting our technique with the wire cutters.

Another reason we are down to our last draw stuff is because ever since Tula started dancing at the peep show she has been going behind my back and trading the designer jackets and dresses in for stripper clothes instead of money. The other day I was digging through one of the big blue plastic bins of clothes of the house we crash at for something to wear to my job interview and I kept pulling out handfuls of sparkly four-inch skirts and spandex halter tops.

"Damnit Tula, I have a job interview at a nice restaurant."

"I'm sure they wouldn't mind you washing dishes in this," Tula said, picking up some purple hot pants off the floor and slingshoting them at me.

Even at the vintage store she wanted to spend our cash on a pair of boots she was obsessing over. And we didn't even make that much. "Man, we gotta stop stealing so much crap from the Gap, nobody wants this stuff and it's also totally embarrassing," I had mumbled to her when the buyer went to cut our check. The buyers are always some really amazing fashion goddess-type girls who mesmerize me and I forget to even blink as they coldly accept or reject something, which starts to feel like a game of *She loves me, she loves me not.*

I was shoving all the rejects back into the garbage bags and Tula was snapping around in these gold-heeled boots that she wanted to trade our lousy thirty-dollar check for, saying, "Hey, I'm not even allowed to wear street shoes at my job." But really she already has work shoes and I need that money for laundry and boxes of Mac n' Cheese and for taking the bus to look for jobs, and I don't trust Tula at keeping the dancing job, especially since it keeps her there all night when she'd rather be sitting with the boys at the bar.

"Look I'll get the boots for you another day, ok," I said, shooting her a look. She knew what I meant by that so she gave in and reluctantly unzipped the shiny gold vinyl that was suctioned around her calves. Back in *Shoplifting 101* (which is what I call the anti-shoplifting class my probation officer sent me to once when I was caught, because really it was a class where I learned a lot of tricks), the first thing everybody did was put the desks in a big circle and we went around telling our stories of exactly what we did and how we got caught. One of the funniest stories was this girl who walked into Ross barefoot and came out in a new pair of heels. She got caught and we all laughed about how she went to Juvi barefoot, but hey, I've secretly always wanted to try shoplifting barefoot.

On the bus back down Haight I showed Tula the flyer for the girl party and she was like, "You know I hate that lesbian shit." It was true that back in suburbia me and Tula weren't really friends with any of the dykes that hung out at the coffee shop parking lot where we smoked cigarettes and drank our 40s while waiting to find out about parties or shows. The dykes were weird to us; they all hung out in a small group and took turns dating each other like they were interchangeable cookie cutters, all with the same wife beater, cropped hair and sandals. They knew I had always been into girls and that Tula and I were fucking but they never invited us to their parties, and they made it pretty obvious that we weren't real queers if it wasn't stamped in rainbow letters across our foreheads.

But I knew San Francisco was different. There were queers everywhere and they were even the glamour girls working at the vintage store, or the nerdy girls in cat eye glasses at the bookstores, or the shaggy-haired bike-riding girls that rode by me. They were all over and the pent-up girl fuck in me was dying to figure out how to navigate their world. So yeah, I would try to talk Tula into it, say, *C'mon it's called Rebel Girl so there gots to be hot punk rock chicks there*, but I'll go alone if I have to, hang out shyly in the corner and drink my beer.

Under the fluorescent light in the donut shop bathroom I put on some tinted lip-gloss, roll the cuffs of my black Dickies down, and shove my beanie in my hoodie pocket. I rumple my hair that was flattened by the beanie and crunch its stiffness between my fingers. We bleached out my hair at the beginning of summer just before moving to the city. The peroxide burned Tula's hands cause we didn't have any rubber gloves. After, Tula had this bumpy white rash and my hair was just as strange, all jagged with stiff tips that were more like pointy darts than hair.

I hide the skateboard in a row of bushes lining the sidewalk down the block from the bar where the girl club is. This is an old trick I learned as a minor in my town where you could get your board taken away if you're caught out after curfew. The bush swallows up the board and it stays waiting there for you to come back for it.

The girl walking into the club in front of me makes me want to turn around; her pompadour is even bigger than mine. Her boots slam into the sidewalk with each swagger, and her keys jingle a rhythm against her hip. I don't own any keys but I'd consider collecting fake ones and hooking then on my jeans if that jingle could set off girl gaydar half a block away. My nervousness doubles when it comes to the door girl. Good thing my fake ID has a high success rate, even if it hurts my feelings every time it works because the girl in the picture is really awful looking. I just smile nice and say, "Hey, it's been a good year, ya know?"

In the club I look around the room, girls of all kind slip, sweep, shimmer-sweet, and flicker by me. I go to up to the bar and order a beer and I see a couple girls there that me and Tula had met at the Dyke march, where we basically just went and got stoned and then Tula was bored and wanted to go get cheeseburgers so we left.

"Where's your girlfriend?" The one with the dreads visiting from Canada wants to know.

"She's not my girlfriend."

"Damn, I wish I'd known that the other day, she's so hot."

"Uh-huh," I say, and I think of Tula back at the house, sitting on the window ledge probably with a cigarette in one hand and a beer in the other, wearing her favorite pink and black strappy thrift store dress with fishnets and dirty Converse shoes. She would, of course, be the center of attention, all the guys giving her whatever she asked for and she loving to entertain her guests. Her asymmetrical mouth sideways in her loud laugh, lips lopsided like childhood. When she was barely walking she bit an electrical cord, clamped down on it and probably didn't even want to let go. And her small pointy teeth must have absorbed some of the shiny electric pacifier permanently because whenever they sunk into my collarbone or neck they fried permanent pin-sized marks that my fingers would trace over and over.

At 3 A.M. I'm sitting on the front steps in front of the Fell St. house with this girl—well, woman—named Deez who kept buying me drinks at the club. When the bar was closing she told me that she was impressed that I came to the club by myself but she really didn't think I should leave alone. We took a cab with her friends to the girl bar, which was closed, but one of the friends worked there so we could play pool in the empty bar. The bartender friend made out with her girlfriend the entire time and Deez explained that this was a new girlfriend and that was why they wouldn't stop making out. She told me stuff about the scene, said, "Been here eight years." I concentrated on beating her twice at pool and she leaned back against the bar with an amused smile. She kept shaking her head and saying, "I dunno where you came from but you are real cute."

I put out my cigarette on the porch step. I know that Deez wants to go upstairs and I think it would be fun to fool around with a tough older girl like her but what if Tula got off work early or Blue was back from out of town? And anyways how would I explain to Deez that I live with an old drunk guy for free? I could tell her the whole story about how me and Tula had to get out of that redneck town, so small and hot and paved over with tract homes and concrete that was only good for tagging and skateboarding, and how our friend Krista moved to the city and became a stripper and stayed with a thirty-something-year-old drunk washed-up skater who everyone called Baby Blue, for his watery baby blue eyes, and that he was so wasted all the time that he didn't care about Krista's friends crashing at his house.

Deez would look around the living room where I slept on a single mattress on the floor with Tula—the mattress like a droopy raft floating in a sea of girl clothes, and that big chunk of a mirror we found on the street that was now crusted with a layer of hairspray, glitter, and false eyelashes, and the wall of beer cans around the windowsill. Or all the stuff around the room that Blue's screen-printing company made, the plastic crap, like lamp shades, lunch boxes, and candles with pin-up girls screen-printed on them and boxes of porn picture T-shirts. Naw, somehow I didn't think she would go for it.

"It's convenience," I try to explain to Deez. "He's just a sad man drinking it all away. He likes us girls around and we don't have money yet to get a place."

"Sure, he likes real young cute things around." Deez rolls her eyes. Yeah, she was definitely not like the girls I was used to; girls that got by on a lipstick-pretty face and really fake IDs for free clubs, drinks, and drugs. Even the way Deez lights up another cigarette, cocking her head back with the first drag and one boot stretched over the steps she looks somehow unshakable. "You see, honey, I'd never be in your kinda situation, that dude you stay with wouldn't want me to move in at all. To get in good with him I'd have to bro' down and shit, talk about chicks or sports or some shit, that's how I'd gain his respect."

I sigh, lean back on my elbows, and don't know what to say. Deez reaches over and pets my mess of crunchy hair and then she is kissing me. The kiss is real soft and slow for coming from someone that looks so hard. I kiss her back for a bit, but my mind wanders to the way Tula and I smash our lips into each other like we are two trains colliding. Deez pulls back eventually and says, "I'm just looking out for ya, kid. Sometimes situations like that get sketchy. "

She stands up and looks up at the orangey windows of the house. "I hate him," she says. "I want to egg his house or something." I laugh at how silly that sounds, like when you are a kid that's the worst thing you can get away with and you have to accept it. I'd rather keep my fantasy going, that one morning we'll wake up and find that Blue has choked on drunk vomit in his sleep, taking him out of his drunken sadness. Then we girls could have the whole house to ourselves like pilfering princesses with our very own castle.

Deez is talking about how she takes her dog some mornings to the park around the corner. She says I should meet him sometime. This couple walks up the street looking drunk and wobbly and pointing at the sky. "That's the big dipper right?" The guy asks us and we look up and say, yeah. Then the guy checks us out closer; Deez is holding my hand. While he walks away he clenches his hand tighter around the girl's tight booty-jeaned hips. "I be making sure other brothers aren't getting up on my lady but I guess I should be looking out for the sisters."

I jolt awake in the middle of the night. I forget where I am, forget how I got to this small place with windows smaller than the moon. I can hear Baby Blue yelling in his sleep at the demons behind his eyes. Tula is asleep next to me; she could sleep through anything. My hand slides off the side of the mattress and onto the cold hardwood floor and I feel around for my backpack and grab my Marlboro Reds and sketchbook.

As I smoke I look over at Tula's pale skin glowing in the darkness. Back home her body used to make some kind of sense to me but now it's vague and blurred around the edges—skin is as chilly as the hardwood floors, and I can't get past the usual bored look in her eyes and blank laughter to what is familiar. Like how we used to get tangled up in each other's limbs laying on the couch all day in the den of her mom's house. Tula always had to stay home and baby-sit her little sister's baby. Her sister was seventeen and had dropped out of school but she worked full-time and since Tula didn't have a job their mom made her baby-sit. The baby, who we called Gummy, was really cute; he was half-Asian and would squiggle around everywhere and chew on everything with his gummy mouth and we would lay around all day watching TV or plotting our move to the city.

Sometimes we fucked when the baby was sleeping but mostly Tula would rather fool around at parties or wherever we went drinking. She hated that her sister could call her a dyke or a lesbian. Her sister said it like she was spitting at the end of the sentence, like "Shut up, you *lesbian*." Or "If you don't clean the house I'm telling mom how you're a big ole *dyke*." Once when her sister was really going off Tula threw her full glass of juice at her head and it shattered against the wall. When Tula was real mad the sister always ran upstairs shrieking because the whole family was kind of scared of Tula mad. Now, Tula doesn't seem to get angry at all. Whenever I try to touch her she shrugs me off. She seems to let the guys do whatever they want to her if they bring over what she wants.

What if I could turn Tula into a superhero? I breathe in the smell of my assorted Sharpie pens. She would have red splattering swirls for her hair and an oval mouth. She would have those gold boots she wanted strapped to her like a golden armor. I learned to draw from the graffiti boys at the alternative high school I went to, and I mostly draw hip-hop girls or skater girls with real big pants or spray-can–wielding girls with big cartoon hands spreading up across the paper. If Tula had superhero powers they would be silently lethal, like when the enemy touched her she might crack open and her guts would be toxic. Plutonium and sticky things would ooze from her lips. She would be like a swaying doll of a time bomb waiting till she had the room hypnotized before she detonated.

"I know that I'm going to die young," Tula always insisted. "Go out with a bang." I can even hear it now, so faint beneath the street noise, a soft ticking in her chest, as I curl closer into her sleeping body.

Deez yanks a slobbery tennis ball from her dog's mouth and hurls it across the park. The dog is an orangey brown pit bull that kinda resembled Deez with its half-loveable/half-snarling face. "What are you up to today?" Deez asks. I tell her how I gotta work later and all about the job I just got at a touristy diner. There are two really great things about the place: the pink-skirted waitresses who I work with and the leftover food I can bring home. The second night I worked I brought Tula back a piece of meat. I wish it could have been the round-eyed one with the upturned nose and chunky thighs, swish, swishing past me all night, but it was just a pork chop wrapped in a napkin.

Deez says she's been keeping her eyes out for a room for me. I think about how this morning was, waking up and stepping over people passed out on the floor and searching for a beer can just so I can throw my dirty tampon in the trash. Deez and I sit on a park bench and I tell her all about what's going on with Tula. When I tell her about my plan to go get Tula the boots Deez freaks out. "What the fuck you doing that for? This girl is a bad deal; you need to know that you can't make her happy." I nod and kick the dirt with my skate shoes that are starting to lose all their rubber. "You should be ganking yourself some new shoes." Deez laughs.

At the end of my shift I replace the dishwater-wet pink smock with a white T-shirt that sticks to my skin with damp anticipation. I'm ready to cruise through the cool evening on my still-borrowed board. I think I'll head up Market to Tula's work, turn up Union past all the tourists and ching-changing trolley cars and by then it's too steep so I have to walk. I go up through the arch of the red dragon eyes guarding over the entrance to Chinatown and up toward North Beach. Everything around me shifts into something new with every block.

At Tula's new work Zoëy the door girl is sitting at the front desk, sliding a nail file back and forth. She looks up at me and seems relieved—but still bored—that I'm not just another suit who's come to see strippers, and starts chatting on about some club she and her friends have started throwing that she wants me to come to. I look at the Polaroids of the dancers on the wall by the front door while Zoëy lists off all these DJ names that I have never heard of. In Tula's picture she has a close-lipped smile and a black bobbed wig falling into her face and beneath that her name scrawled in black ink, *I'm not gonna be no plain Jane anymore*. I realize that at this point in our relationship, or whatever you might call it, Tula and I have the same relationship that she has with hundreds of strangers every day; with a little investigation and a handful of quarters they too can long for intimacy all while being kept back at a safe distance.

In the rooms and booths of the club there's a pungent scent that never completely washes away even beneath the strong smell of cleaning supplies. A stickiness coats the floors and the view frame of the smudgy windows that look into the red room. The room looks like a huge fish tank with its bubble of round mirrors. Tula even shines like a goldfish with this body glitter stuff on her skin that we got at the mall the last trip. She is across the room when my screen goes up and all I can see is her mouth moving, as if she is underwater and puffing her lips against the glass. All the girls seem to glow beneath the red light; they sway around each other with glimmering girl wigs and snapping girl eyelashes. Some of these girls I've met back at the house or at the bar, with doll-like faces and wide eyes that seem to be searching for something, they search purses and shot glasses, assholes and nasal passages, wallets and every new set of eyes.

One night at the house they wanted to know why I don't dance. Of course I wanted to make easy money, I told them, but it just wasn't right when Tula got me all dolled up. "She's got zero tits and ass, looks like a little boy," Tula explained.

"Lotsa guys are into that," Trixie said, swirling a blond ringlet tight around her finger and letting it spring loose

Through the glass I watch Tula blow the bangs of the black bobbed wig off her face. I run out of my few quarters so the screen starts to roll down and in the split second before everything goes to black I swear I can see her hands spinning like firecracker sparklers and spraying conductive energy from her fingertips.

Outside the club the bright gray sky blinds me. Sometimes the fog is so thick in this city that I can't even see the skyline and it makes me feel like I could disappear. I sit down on the sidewalk in front of the club and draw in my sketchbook until Tula gets off work.

Tula comes out with Zoëy and they say they want to go to the Mission bars. People go to some bars just for the drugs and both Tula and the skater guys tend to like those ones. Tula and Zoëy link their arms. They have on coats but still wear heels and fishnets. The cars are like spotlights when they stop and let them cross the street, but when I trail a bit behind I practically get run over. When I catch up to them and tell them I'm tired from work and don't want to go to the bar, they just shrug because all they care about is getting there.

In the dark hall closet, the shadows of shoes flicker down the hall beneath the door crack. I sip on the cool mouths of beer bottles and the squeaking of the pen distracts me from the ache in my chest. I wonder if my gold-booted superhero even had a heart would be shaped like a grenade?

When Deez flicks her cigarette she can zing it way across the sidewalk to hit a parked truck. "Show me how to do that," I say. We are standing in front of the girl bar where I met up with her to shoot some pool. I practice my cigarette flick and I see this cute girl on an old rusty bicycle. I ask Deez who the girl is because she knows everyone. "That's Molly," Deez says. "You should for sure hang out with her, she makes a 'zine and would probably be super into your drawings."

Just when I get the nerve to talk to Molly, she hops on her bike and my heart sinks. Deez laughs and squeezes my shoulders. "Don't worry, you will for sure meet her next time."

"Yeah, next time." I smile watching the girl roll away down the slanted street.

I wake up to the door buzzer rattling my head at five in the morning. I go downstairs sleepy and outside the door is Zoëy trying to get a sloppy-looking Tula out of a cab. I run out barefoot to help her and Zoëy says, "We both lost our purses or they got stolen so we don't have keys or money for the cab."

"Sure," I say to Zoëy who is rumored to be a liar with a speed problem, but someone has to pay for the cab so I run back upstairs and creak open the door of Baby Blue's room. He is snoring loudly and under the red light of one of the small pin-up girl lamps that spin in a circle flickering shapes across the room I see Krista wrapped tightly around him, as if she could ever hold him tight enough to stop his night tremors. I spy Blue's wallet on the desk, grab it, and tiptoe out of the room.

While I pay the cab Zoëy tells me how some guys bought them all these drinks and then all she remembers is that they were at this party and she thinks she got some bad drugs because she thought Tula left with this other guy, but when she was leaving she found Tula passed out half-naked in a room where these sketchy guys were still up playing poker. The more Zoëy rambles on, the madder I get because I know she was probably not watching out for Tula at all. "Stop fucking whispering about me you assholes," Tula slurs.

I shove some more cab fare in Zoëy's face so she won't ask to stay over. I can't handle her sneaky little eyes.

Upstairs Tula sits on the coffee table and shivers. "Where are my tights?" she asks, looking down at her bare legs that are all goose pimpled. I grab the blanket from the mattress and try to put it over her but she just holds it in her lap. "I don't remember anything," she says. Her bottom lip starts to quiver like leftover electricity is trying to get out.

"Listen, Tula, I think we should leave here."

"Where can we go?" Tula mumbles into the blanket as she rubs her eyes. I sit down on the mattress next to her and try to assure her that I've got it all figured out. We'll travel across the country and jump on trains or hitchhike on old highways, make money screen-printing T-shirts or selling stolen clothes on the road.

Tula moves the blanket from her eyes, now dark pools of smudged makeup. She gets up and paces the small room, says, "Why don't you just admit it? You think I'm gonna end up back home with a baby crawling all over me, dontchya?" She kicks at a pile of Bettie Page lunchboxes with her boots, denting the cheap plastic. I want her to stop spinning around the room but I feel like I have helium hands and I can't do anything to keep her still. I try to pull the blanket over my head but she comes over and starts tugging it and then grabs at my clothes like a frenzied little animal. Her pupils are small and hard like pomegranate seeds as she glares down at me. I realize this is the first time I've seen her angry in so long and so I let her do what she is doing, mash her lips against mine and eventually shove her hand into me, following her own erratic earthquake of a rhythm. She doesn't really know how to fuck a girl so there's no way to anticipate what direction she is gonna come from. I grab the sides of the mattress as it bangs against the wall. Morning rush hour has begun so already it feels like the bed is nailed down in the center of the street below, where the cars shoot off the freeway off-ramp and rattle the windows. But it is Tula who makes the beer cans fall from the windowsill, hit the floor one by one, small crashes oozing leftover juices.

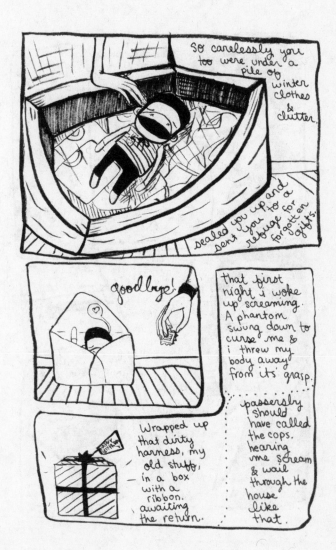

Laundry Day

Robin Akimbo

Laundry is always a commitment. Depending on the severity of my agoraphobia that week, it can be a simple task; time to devote to a long-distance phone call conversation I've been putting off; or, at best, a self-check-in ritual. I can get away with doing it only once a month because I have so much clothes and underwear that my makeshift closet is in a perpetual state of disarray regardless. I feel thoroughly proud of myself for completing the mammoth quest, comparable to nothing other than perhaps moving. I have a giant suitcase on wheels and a small duffel bag full of dirty clothes. No car. The hike demands all of my strength to prevent tripping upward as I ascend Bernal Hill to the nearest Laundromat. Fear renders the expedition: I not only *leave* my house, but will be in *public* for a few hours, a nearly impossible feat.

I indulge in my agoraphobia, believing it justified. It's a side effect of city living, and many girls know it. It's the You-know-what? I'm-just-not-"strong"-enough-to-cope-

with-sexual-harassment-today-asshole setback, and it's real.
But I am forced to snap out of my triggered neurosis to do
the chore that can no longer wait. I have a show coming up
in a few days, six classes in school, three shifts at work, and
I joke that I need a housekeeper 'cause I can't manage my life
anymore. And it shows. I need a tutor, an assistant, hell, why
not a manager—no, a patron, let's dream big.

It is a humbling experience, lugging my two massive
laundry bags up the Bernal Hill from Folsom St., requiring
serious strategy. Within three blocks on the same street there
is the typical San Francisco phenomenon of crossing three
different socioeconomic realities in less than ten minutes.
Starting with the confusing area of Victorians that from a
distance look like the Victorians of the postcards, but up
close are rotting shells owned by slumlords so crafty they
could only reside in the Mission. These places house all
forms of pestilence and danger: mold, lead, and decaying
electrical wires, to name a few. An interesting alternative to
the touristy mural walks of the neighborhood would be the
activity of spotting how many houses actually have a metal
plaque warning screwed between their doorways, claiming:
WARNING: This Area Contains Chemicals Known to The
State of California to Cause Cancer and Birth Defects or
Other Reproductive Harm. Housing laws require this. The
property owners here think a formal warning to the tenants
equivalent or better to reparations. These buildings tend to
occupy mostly Mexicans and a few queer stragglers of
various racial backgrounds, the latter accused of gentrifying
the neighborhood, though they know full well the yuppies

who own their houses are the ones who've installed automatic garages to protect their cars, who occupy the newer condos around the corner.

I am somewhat miscellaneous, though am often mistaken for a sixteen-year-old neighborhood girl because of my defaulted comfort level and the way I dress. This may grant me safe passage under certain circumstances, but my politics get me nowhere—I've reclaimed a valuable amount of entitlement around things like personal space and the simple right to exist, rendering it difficult to fully adhere to the laws of the land when taken out of context. Though I may sometimes blend, I am identifiably prey here. The acknowledgment offered by my glance in the direction of the potential predator is self-protective—not cause I want it, yo. When unaware, I will instinctively or habitually look down at the pavement as I walk, to make myself smaller. When I see the Latin girls doing this it makes me sad—the only reason I notice it in myself.

So before I leave my house, I select what to wear. What on earth is a) not dirty, and b) nonconfrontational? It's oppression at work people, I the unwilling participant. Therapists and friends alike have told me that I am adjusting wisely for survival's sake, a chameleon that's no fool, and I agree, though it's hard not to want to die nobly in the line of fire— uncompromising, teeth bared. What disturbs me most is lamenting the fanciful philosophies of my once more intentionally punk existence, so deliberate about being as condemning as possible. If I was feeling invisible I would dye my dreads Pillar Box Red; couple a miniskirt with matching platform boots; makeup to scare a banshee. Just Fucking Try It—my mantra, with every stompy step.

Block two, neighborhood two—where permission is most required. I am feeling defiant today. Today's a good day, they can tell I'm way more on their side of the scale than some weird artist, 'cause I am brown and tired and have no shame—I am hauling my own massive bags, and it's not for once, it's always. I am uncomfortable to the point where they are trying not to embarrass *me* by staring too intently. Great! We're on the same page! The more normal I think I'm acting, the more I cringe at my self-consciousness, for we have so much in common, and then we don't. The "They" of which I speak are the people of color sentenced to the projects that fringe the edge of the Mission. They hang out, go to the corner, get the updates, work on their cars. Their buildings are new. They are pissed that they live there, but it reinforces not only the idea others have of them but ideas they have of themselves. Being part of a community, and a tough one at that. Expected to do nothing, treated as nothing, rewarded for being clever, street-smart, profiting off of the law's ignorance. I would hang out, too—watch TV all day. Ambition: you have to know it to miss it. You have to have had access in the first place. I want to high-five them for being so styly; undefeated in the art of impeccable color coordination, right down to the hair accessories; a different color of sneaks for every day. Yeah girl. The boys talk louder for my benefit; I nod as I walk by, and look up to notice satellite dishes in almost every window.

Approaching an intersection, I move my eyes again to

diffuse the intensity of territorial voyeurism, now having approached the several scattered, debatably illegal Mexican laborers. The various ways a city's diverse society can create its own Band-Aid solutions for what the city itself won't provide always blow me away. You see this all the time here: the resourceful nature of San Francisco's street residents, compared to the total lack of creativity of city management. They've pretty much left recycling up to the homeless/addict population, giving them the job of collecting cans, keeping their hands full, so they can't think about the fact that a real job would require a fraction of the physical energy required to sustain a food/drug habit so acute. Course, they'd be playing by someone else's rules. But they already are. And here, on Cesar Chavez, these strong-shouldered laborers, young and old, are stationed, hoping for an opportunity to be of use for easy cash. They lean against the off-white wall, work boots splayed, pants covered in paint, arms crossed in wait for a truck to stop in an instant. It is necessary for them to reclaim some pride, to deflect from their obvious, displayed need. They look at me as they would entertainment, subtly smirking and elbowing each other in Spanish. They reign it in as I glance back a second time, knowingly—they can't be sure I don't understand—and I get braver as the light's about to change . . . the sixteen-second electronic white man walking countdown, the crossing of what used to be Army St. but is now Cesar Chavez, on the way up the hill.

It is October, almost dark at seven o'clock. The Laundromat's bright lights are predictably disarming. There are two or three Mexican mothers chatting and waiting for their clothes in the dryers, watching their kids haphazardly, and a youngish white couple comes in behind me. I often fantasize about learning Spanish—at least learn how to fight in Spanish if I could only wash my clothes more frequently. I could absorb the language of the obvious plots and unnecessary drama of the screaming telenovelas into my subconscious. Maybe then I'd be able to hold my own on the street. I'd have to be in there several times a week to get anywhere, but I liked the idea—getting hooked on the sounds of the stories, and realizing one day that you understand everything that's being said in Spanish on the TV. I could rip it up with the best of them.

I go for the giant sixteen-quarter spinner, and a small child with black hair stares at my ratty mane. He loses interest in my aesthetic soon, and returns to a small game he's playing with his brother. I nearly stumble over a black bag the size of my own full of hockey equipment and think I'm hallucinating, 'cause I haven't seen one of those since visiting my family in Canada. The proprietor of the bag is the male half of the white couple, a medium-sized blond in his early thirties. He ignores me, his wife within view, the same medium height, she is squawking by the change machine. He squawks back, and this is how I know they are married, or at least live together in a long-term manner: they can barely leave each other's side, not in an affectionate way, but in a micro-managing, curious as to the job the other is doing at whatever task is at hand kind of way, and their general tone is one of endless bickering. They seem unaware of this and are not taking note of their noise or offense to each other. Now sitting on the bench trying to read, I am mildly engrossed in my book for the duration of their dispute, distracted by the mounted TV in the corner and the rest of my wash cycle.

I crave a latté but the café's closed. I console myself with Cheetos and Gatorade from the corner store and return to put my clothes in the dryer. Smug with my treats, I read some more, easier now that the white couple has piped down. The Mexican women and their children have long exited the place, and it is just us three for a while. My gigantic load is divided between two dryers, and naturally some things dry faster than others. I have never been a sorter, neither in color, nor in fabric—so twenty minutes into everything I interrupt the rotating rainbow to detangle the colored nylons from the moist towels, and the polyester dresses from the damp denim. Removing and throwing the most obviously dry items into the wheeled basket, I begin to fold. The warm clothing is a comfort in my arms.

A new presence enters the establishment, and the general vibe lets me guess the gender. I keep about my business as the intensity builds, a sick opera of my paranoia. Wanting to assure it is not just my imagination, I glance over and yes—it is a very large male, looking like a rightful prison convict, and he is a little too aware of me. My intuition honed; correct. There are various kinds of crazy in this town, but the two that most commonly raise the hairs on my neck are a) crackhead—don't look them in the eyes because it's the closest you can get to confronting Satan, and b) homicide rapist. I assume it's b), because he's keeping his mouth shut. My tactic at this moment is denial of his existence. Whatever.

Fold, fold, ignore. I am doing my laundry, underwear in a pile, shirts, tights, whatever else. I have a purpose; his eyes are not burning into me. He isn't so threatening, seems to have been in earlier, because he has laundry in the wash, and is now transferring it to the dryer . . . beside mine . . . beside my clothes . . . is that really necessary? Yes, apparently.

He is finding ways of being in the direct path of my gaze so I have no choice but to look up, a furious effort to get my attention. I guess he really needs me to look at him. If I do maybe it will diffuse this, maybe that's his only objective. I look up. He's completely fucking nuts in a murderous way. Now he's seen my soul, and he wants it. Olive skin carved with neck tattoos, face inexplicably mean. Thinning black hair; rotting sweats. He is poised on the bench across from me like the Italian dads back in Rosemont: sitting on their stoops, one leg up; a macho come-and-get-it display. The present specimen belongs to a group of psycho types that insist they are my instant boyfriends, who miss the irony of my rebel wear and the authenticity of my disinterest and think, oh yes here's a feline stung enough to cope with the level of danger I exude. They yell at me on Mission St., follow me from car to car on the BART train, barricade me with their giant trucks when I'm on my bike. Something about me is particularly familiar or desirable—brown, femme, scrappy—which makes them think "up for it." Up for a serious dance with violence. My existence at once confrontational and tempting. This hateful paradox frequently subjects me to what I call "rape face": an expression that emotes fury at the nerve of my choosing to exist so defiantly, and an attraction that wants to consume, then kill it. All this can be read at a glance. It makes leaving my house a very bad idea.

I think I will catch him looking at me. The bench he's positioned on is no more than six feet away, so I bravely lift my eyes once more, this time with twisted lips, and no—he is not looking at me, he is staring at my underwear. My beautiful collection of multicolored, patterned, dainty, girly, underwear. Overtly violated, I faux-casually scoop them up and throw them in the black suitcase on the floor, trying not to show humiliation and fear. He is dangerously close to me. I am "safe" only for the two potential witnesses in the room: this whole scenario is framed by the bickering white couple, serving to stir up the energy of the place, however utterly oblivious to my dilemma. They are busily folding and chatting on the other table; they'd have to be hit over the head to notice any silent cold war between two people of color. I am grateful for their presence however, because I become suddenly and painfully aware that otherwise I'd be alone. With an obvious lunatic. I decide to stave off terror until I can get my laundry and go. He's not going to control my every move, I insist to myself.

I notice again the safety of the couple, beyond entitlement. I envy the wife, who whether she needs it or not possesses the relaxed ease of one who has a bodyguard. I wonder if she even realizes or has ever had to deal with the level of harassment I have, and if she's grateful. I think of the days as recently as the '20s when it was frowned upon for women to be alone in public. "Societal control!" we scream, and there is nothing radical about being protected, treated as though it's necessary, accommodating male violence—or is there? I don't care what it means politically, I think to myself—I'm tired. Sometimes being alone, although I'm stubbornly so, is too hard.

Enough is enough: the cycle's done. I go with the basket on wheels to pull it out. The Opportunist chooses this precise moment to verify the state of his laundry, conveniently located in the neighboring machine. You suck. I pull mine out fast, dumping it down, make sure I have everything, and am very resentful that we were practically touching while I'm trying to get the job done. Wheeling the basket to my table I pick up the pace, but pretend I am in my own little world. Then the unthinkable happens.

Whether he retrieved them seconds ago from my basket as we were side by side, or they actually fell on the floor without my noticing, he now possesses a pair of my underwear in his hand, and proceeds to *throw them at me*. With a smirk he turns around immediately and begins a status promenade—this brutal insult his idea of play—attempting to rile me up to get some kind of reaction. Because I've been anticipating something I skip right over the fear stage and grow straight into blind rage. I am ready to kill him.

In a few milliseconds I travel through every time in my life I nearly died at the hands of some kind of violent situation, and I start breathing through my nostrils like a bull, jaw half agape, shoulders rising. I see the giant laundry table overturned, I see hands, my hands, wrapped tightly around his thick neck, and I am strangling him to death, kicking my legs around his waist, he is throwing me around, but I am driven by a rage that is insatiable, a fury that makes me spit. His hands on my underwear, I can't believe it—that Fuck. *I'm not ready to die today,* I proclaim internally, now with a little more oxygen in my brain. I would die for sure. I'm not ready to. Breathe, calm, breathe, don't show him you even noticed, you didn't, don't talk, put your things away slowly . . . slowly. . . .

Rendering him invisible was my survival instinct. I chose Freeze over Flee or Fight. Like some kind of giant predator cat, my refusal to react caused him to lose interest in his prey. He'd been pawing me, and upon realizing that I was already dead, gave up—circled the room one last time, and left. I waited till he was out of sight, praying that he wasn't lurking in the dark, but knew in my gut he was gone. I hurriedly threw the rest of my clothes in the bags, did a final check for any lingering items, and left.

Going down the hill is always easier, and in a way darkness affords me more of a veil. Motivated by adrenaline, I walked tall, viciously mad, but happy I won the breath of another day. Appeased only by the thought of how I would tell the story, who I would call first, trying not to cry, not to let the shame sink in. I was in one piece. Grateful for the darkness. It's harder for them to see me coming.

Snow Fight

Mecca Jamilah Sullivan

This old white nigga starts talking and everybody shuts up real tight for a second. Then they start screaming, "*Eeeeeh! Eeeeeeh!*," cheering like on the playground watching Pito and Slimminy try to murder each other one on one, or when Sonjra and Ana-Rosario skipped Mr. Dominic's math class to go snatch clothes from on two-fifth street and rocked their new Baby Phat jeans straight through eighth period still with the plastic lock tags on. They ain't even hear what the old white nigga said, and I'm not gonna front, I didn't really hear it either, it was so noisy. I was just so surprised to see him open his mouth, and even more surprised to see the snow come out. And when he said "*shit!*" forget it. It was a wrap. I always wondered what one of those random old white niggas on the train would do if you touched them or winked at them, or rubbed your ass up on them one time when it was crowded or something. I thought maybe they would turn pink and start sweating and maybe pull on they necktie like that old video for

"Baby Got Back," Sir Mix-a-Lot, I think, when he sees the black girl with the phatty and it hits him too close, closer than white people like to go.

But your boy didn't do any of that. All he did was clear his throat and say "*HEY!*" real loud like Principal Scaprioni does at assemblies when Light-skin Chris and them or some other niggas is actin loud, singing R. Kelley songs to the girls in the back row. Scaprioni screams "HEY!" louder and they sing louder, going from the Chocolate Factory album and Step in the Name of Love straight back to some shit I can't even remember the title about "*your booody's caaallin fooor me.*" Scaprioni says "*HEY*" real loud, not loud as five or ten niggas singin' to cute girls, but who got the microphone? You can feel his voice shaking the walls from out the speakers, if you not talking you can even feel it under your feet.

Me, I sit with my homegirl Patricia and she teaches me words in Spanish. When Chris and them act up she tells me they acting mad *bobo*, and when Scaprioni starts sweating like the white dude on the video, his fat face shining like a greasy ham hock, she says "*que parece cerdo.*" I laugh, cause my homegirl is funny, and cause I like how things she say in Spanish be so similar to what I think in English. I don't know, shit like that be real funny to me. Sometimes, if Dominique showed up to school that day and decided to sit with us instead of her flavor-of-the-week nigga, she bite on her braids how she do and say some Jamaican shit 'bout "*dat de man a puar wharff daawg!*" but I'm not good at understanding all that. She make me laugh in the same way, though, for the simple fact that when me and Patricia went to her house, she had ox tails and fried fish and hush puppies, but her whole family called it "ox tail" with no "s," and they call hush puppies "*festival*," and when Patricia asked what kind of fish it was, Dominique said it was "salt fish," but Patricia said she coulda swore it was *bacalao*. Crazy how shit could be different as night and day, then turn out to be the same damn thing just in a different language or a different sauce. I don't know, I just laugh.

Principal Scaprioni doesn't usually have to shake the ground more than once, even though they say 155 is the worst school in the city. They only say that because them dumb-ass niggas Andrew and Alex put on some black T-shirts and brought heat to school last year, their senior year, okay, in April, not even two months before their graduation, and tried to shoot the nose off the sphinx statue in the lobby, talking 'bout "*THIS IS POLITICAL!*" Now we have to go through metal detectors every time we come in and out—before first period, after fourth period, after lunch, after eighth. The line be down the street, almost to the train station. And still they expect us to get to class on time. What is that? And now we 'posed to be these badass kids, meanwhile the worst shit that happens on a regular day is some dumb-ass, bobo-ass, wharff daawg-ass niggas singing "Sex Me!" to a bunch of eighth-grade girls who can't even be bothered.

Well, I guess that's not true, depending on whose side you look at it from. What shit does go down at 155 is cause they send these teachers, white girls, okay, whose names are probably Mary-Jane and Becky-Sue, to come teach us, mad heads, like thirty-five if everybody would show up, offa three or four books and a halfa piece of chalk. Even when these niggas have the book, half of them can't read worth shit so what are they gonna do? Act up. I feel bad for the Mary-Janes sometimes. September they be really trying, lazy blond hair all combed up, button-down shirts and shit. They come in with all these books they photocopied, and crayon-colored name tags they make to show us they really want to learn our names. By June they be done got hit by some stupid nigga in the arm or the leg, had they ass pinched, been cursed out by some stank-ass female, then cursed out the whole class themselves, cried, and cried some more. Or if not they just broke out before they had the chance. Then I think harder and don't feel sorry at all. They go home to Long Island, the Hamptons or some shit. I go home to 143rd.

The Mary-Janes don't know what to do with us but Scaprioni knows how to shut niggas up. On the news and in the movies they front like principals are some bitch-ass people who just love the kids so much but can't find any way to control them. Picture that. Scaprioni is not scared of a damn body. He is quick to throw you out of the auditorium, or your classroom, or his office, or wherever, and send you right down to the glass box in the lobby with the security guard. (There's two, and people say they are both licensed police officers. I don't know about all that, but I know they have guns and that's all I really need to know.) If it's the white security guard, you're lucky. He just makes you sit in the box with your eyes closed so you can't make faces to any of your peoples that might pass by. But if it is the black nigga, it's a wrap for you. He will sit you with your back to the door and shove a book under your face, and he will tell you you better not touch it for any reason other than to turn the page. He hem niggas up with books like *They Came Before Columbus*, about black people been in America earlier than the pilgrims, or *Cultura Afrocaribeña*, about Dominicans and Puerto Ricans really came from Africa and just try to front. One time Dominique got caught fucking some Haitian nigga under the counter in the cafeteria and when they found them they got sent straight to the box (nobody even called Scaprioni). Well it was the black guard, and he sewed them both up tight. She had to read a book about *When Chicken-heads Come Home to Roost*, and the Haitian nigga got stuffed up with *The Life of Pierre Toussaint*.

That nigga does not play for real. You will be stuck up in that box with nothing to look at but either some long-ass book or the shot-up sphinx statue, which still has its white people nose on cause the dumb niggas couldn't aim for shit and shot a hole in the front left paw instead. That statue is mad ugly, too. They say it used to be blue and gold and yellow, but I can't figure out where cause the paint is all the way chipped off and it's just a nasty-ass brown now, same ugly color as the classroom doors, same color as our desks, same color as most of us. Between the book and the sphinx, you better look at that book. And the black guard, if he even catches you with your eyes above book level for a few seconds, he will keep you there in that glass box till the building closes. And that's not till seven-thirty, way after everyone in the playground been went home, or wherever.

I'ma be real with you. I like staying late at school, if it's warm. In the beginning and the end of the year, we have a really nice time. Niggas play ball shirts and skins, females watch and try to look cute, talk about shit. When we don't have to wear jackets it's like a fashion show for the ones that have money like that. Even the ones that don't, we can watch. It's a nice time too because we can say whatever we want. With everybody out there in the warm times, we can be loud and curse and do whatever the fuck. Lunch isn't like that cause we all have different lunch hours, depending on your class and your schedule. After school it's everybody together and there's too many niggas for Scaprioni and the Mary-Janes to do a damn thing about us, really, other than try to make us leave. Plus, I like the way the air feels on the playground when it's not so cold. The playground's big, you know, and there's no buildings next to it except the school on one side. It's mad open. I like that.

When it's warm, not like now, niggas be runnin' around the courtyard and dancing crazy. Dominique and Patricia and me maybe start a game of double Dutch, and sometimes even some of the ninth-grade girls will jump in, and we will all sing the double Dutch songs we used to sing back in the P.S. days, back when we thought cursing was some hot shit: "*1, 2, my boyfriend wants to do me, 2, 3, he wants to fuck my coochie. . . .*" We sing loud cause we can say whatever we want, cause it be so loud out there that nobody can hear, and it's so many of us that couldn't nobody do shit even if they could hear.

And plus when it's warm and you chill outside you can just

listen to people speak their languages. It gets so uncomfortable having to talk to the Mary-Janes and Becky-Sues all day, for those of us who try. Talking like you're reading from a book or some shit, like wearing a turtleneck sweater, how it stuffs up your throat. After school when it's warm, none'a that. Niggas talk like how they fuckin' talk: "This bitch" this and "yo, son" that. The Haitians talk their African French that is so pretty, and the Jamaican girls go on and on so fast I have to get Dominique to translate for me just so I can know what's happening.

In the wintertime, like now, it's different. It be so cold outside, only the straight-up bobos and wharff daawgs stand around the playground smoking cigarettes. Everybody else takes it to the train. That's when me and Patricia say bye, cause she lives on the A and I take the 1-9. Me and Dominique do us, though. We sit close as we can get to the middle of the train and listen to the Washington Heights niggas fill up the whole seven cars with loud-ass Spanish: "*Eres preciosa, amor, es una placer. . . .*" This scraggly-looking Dominican nigga is trying to spit game to a light-skinned girl. "*¿Eres freshman?*" She don't seem to know how to respond, I guess she's too young.

Down at the other end of the car they are talking so loud I can't hear a damn thing, they laughing and running their mouths 'bout "*¡Culiquitaka ti, culiquitaka ta!*" and "*¡Diablo, que'esa vaina!*" I don't know exactly what they're saying, but it's loud as hell and it sounds like they having a good time. Dominique is, too, talking to some nigga I have never seen, so I just sit quietly and do me, try to pick more words out the air.

Then I notice this old white nigga, his back all bent over like a pterodactyl or some shit, this *Jurassic Park* nigga, face all up in a newspaper. He's not making no noise, but his lips are moving fast as the keys on one of those old-ass type-writers, and I am wondering how long he's gonna ignore all this nigga loudness bumping up against him.

When the doors open at 125th, Light-skin Chris and some other nigga jump out the door, and I think that's weird cause Chris live on my block and we both get off at 145th. But then he comes back into the train with a handful of snow and throws it cross the whole car and hits Slimminy right on his neck. Everybody is like "Ooooh!," and niggas start laughing. The train makes that doorbell noise to let you know the doors are about to close, but Slimminy sticks his little foot between them and reaches out, the doors click and bang against his foot like they don't know what to do, till then he comes back in with a whole armful of snow. Now it's on. Everybody's laughing and cheering in no language at all really. Some girls in the middle of the car reach out there, too, and start flicking snow at each other. The door bells keep ringing and niggas keep blocking the doors, reaching out and throwing big-ass handfuls of dirty snow at each other. Then I catch it. And I'm glad right then that I am the kind of person that watches shit insteada getting caught up in it. Light-skin Chris was aiming for Slimminy, but his right hand slipped down the pole he was hanging from. He lost his balance, and the old white nigga got caught in the face with a clump of nasty gray snow. Chris looked like he saw his mama ghost coming for him.

"HEY!," like Principal Scaprioni, and everyone shuts up quick, like if he was gonna send them to the glass box or expel them. Then, I don't know, everybody starts cheering, screaming eight times louder than before, like if the Knicks would win a championship, like that. Like this was the funniest, best shit in the world. This old white nigga, the only one on the train fulla mad rowdy, laughing negroes, and he gets caught in the face with snow, and what was he gonna do? Niggas cracking up. Then he said something: "something-something, *SHIT!*" And it was over. People was dying, laughing so hard. Dominique was biting her braids hard now, looking like she 'bout to piss herself. The door bells rang again and nobody stopped them this time, everybody caught up in laughing so hard. The snow fell out old boy's mouth and niggas laughed some more. They kept laughing after that and went back to doing their thing, just a little more loud and a little more happy.

But you know, I watched. And I'm glad, too, cause with everything that went down, the funniest shit to me, the part of this story that nobody else even knows, was the way your boy tried so hard to keep his typewriter lips straight while everybody was laughing. It was me, just me, I was the only one that caught this old white nigga stretching his face over his teeth and scrunching up his neck and his eyes just to keep from laughing with us. I laughed hard then, real low in my stomach, cause I never woulda guessed that after all that, even this old white nigga himself would have an urge to smile. I don't know, shit like that is real funny to me.

T-Ten
Chelsea Starr

My grandma sent me twenty bucks for my birthday which is the most money I've ever had at one time in my entire life and you'd think it would be a happy thing, getting twenty dollars in the mail. But really, it's a huge bummer to not just get an actual present. A present would have been mine to keep, whereas money is my mom's to borrow and never to pay back. So the only thing to do after opening the mail is to go to Fred Meyer right away and spend it before my mom comes home from work. She'll be pissed that I spent the money instead of surrendering it to her. "You're so selfish," she'll say. "It makes me sick. They're going to turn off the electricity on Monday and all you can think about is yourself. I would've paid you back," she'll say, "but no. You just couldn't wait, could you? With you it's always 'me me me.'" I think back to last year when Grandma sent ten dollars, which I was promptly made to fork over "for bills." It had been depressing to see a birthday come and go without a cake, a party, or even one present and I'm not going to let that happen again this year.

I say to my twin sister, "H-he-h-h-h-hey, l-l-let's go to Fred Meyer and spend our b-birthday money." She is hesitant, knowing the hell that will break loose upon our mother's return from work. She suggests that we call Mom at work and ask first. "N-n-no way!" I say. "P-PLEASE d-don't call Mom." I convince her not to call our Mom, but I can't get her to come with me to the store. My sister's real opposed to getting yelled at and getting the shit beat out of her, so sometimes it's hard to get her to take certain risks. I go alone, which I know will bode even worse for me later with my mom as she extols my sister's selfless virtues while pocketing her cash.

On my way to Fred Meyer, I think, *I'm SOOOO glad there's no school today.* I'm sick of school. Last week was the worst. I hate my teacher. Her name is Mrs. O'Connor. She's skinny and young and dresses very preppy like Alex P. Keaton on *Family Ties,* and even has the same haircut he does. She has a husband and HE has the haircut, too. I know this because I saw him when he came to school on Valentine's Day to bring her flowers and a big heart-shaped box of candy. Everyone was hoping she'd break open the box of candy and share it with the class but instead she put it in the drawer in her desk. Stingy bastard. All day long I kept thinking about that candy heart in her desk.

In the afternoon everyone was out on recess except for me and this girl because we were inside on detention. Mrs. O'Connor went to take a bathroom break and then Angela and I were alone in the classroom and I swear I could hear that candy heart a-beating. Th-thump. Th-thump. It was excruciatingly difficult for me to restrain myself from busting right into it. Mrs. O'Connor would have known it was me, though, and she already hates me enough. She always looks down her nose at me like I'm the most disgusting thing she's ever seen, and she's never once been nice to me. In fact, she goes out of her way to make things hard for me. In our classroom, the desks are arranged in the shape of a U so that everyone else can see everyone else, and do you know what she did to me for the entire month of March? She put my desk in the middle of the U so the whole class could help her "keep an eye on me," because I never do my work and spend all day doodling and writing notes to myself. It was really awful being on my own little island in the middle of the room with twenty-eight pairs of eyes on me all the time. I mentioned it to my mom, who is not at all the sort of person to involve herself with school affairs, and even she thought it was messed up. She called the school and said, "That's cruel and unusual punishment. You better put my kid's desk back with the other kids."

If you don't pay attention in class or you don't turn in your homework, Mrs. O'Connor puts your name on the board. After that, she'll put a check mark next to it for each additional infraction. If you have your name on the board with one or more checks next to it, you have to stay in during recess. My name was put up on the second day of school and has stayed there all year. It's been so long since I went out for recess, I can barely remember what the playground looks like. If I had to draw a diagram of it, I'm sure I'd get it all wrong.

I keep planning to turn over a new leaf and start doing my homework. I bring home my math book thinking, *Tonight I am actually going to open up this book and actually DO my homework*. But then I get home and I don't want to do it right away. Later. I'll do it later. I play outside for a while. Catch up with the neighbor kids. Go over to Aunt Marlene's to see if I can have some of their dinner. Then I come home and the math homework is looming over my head like a dark cloud. *I think, I really gotta DO something about this.* But then *Mr. Belvedere* is on. Okay, I'll just watch one episode of *Mr. Belvedere* and then I'll do my homework. But what do you know—it's back-to-back episodes and then *Benson* is on. And then we're right into prime time with *Punky Brewster*. I love that show, even though Punky is a bad actress. She's always crying, and it's always SO FAKE. Like the episode where the Challenger explodes. She comes home from school and she's telling Henry about it and she says, "We were all watching it together on TV. It went up into the sky and then it just exploded right in front of our eyes." Henry says, "What did you do then?" Here comes the dramatic part: "Well," she says, "some of the kids cried." Long dramatic pause. ". . . I was one of them." And now her little face is all scrunched up and she's crying and her face is all wet with tears. Not just tear streaks, we're talking ALL WET. Like they took a spray bottle and just spritzed her whole face down. SO FAKE, right? So fake. I still love that show, though. I love Punky's outfit. I love her best friend Cherry. I love her room with the flowers painted all over the walls and her garden lounge chair bed that tips up and down and even has an umbrella. I wish that was my room. After *Punky Brewster* it's time for *Perfect Strangers*. That Balki Bartoko-mous is SO FUNNY. My sister and I really crack up during that show. I think it is our favorite.

With so many good shows on TV, before I know it five hours have gone by and it's late at night and I think, *Oh my gosh! It's nighttime! I have to do my math!!!* So I brush all the crumbs and cigarette ashes off the kitchen table and sit down with my math book. But then I can't find a piece of paper. Or I can find a piece of paper but I don't remember how to do the math problems. Or I do one problem and then fall asleep with my face in the book. Or my mom comes home from work and says, "It's midnight! What are you doing?! Go to bed!" It's always something, and there I am again the next day at school without my homework, praying that Mrs. O'Connor won't call on me when we're correcting our papers. Of course she does, though. She always does. "What did you get for #8?" she'll say. I'll look down at my fingernails and shrug my shoulders. "You don't know, huh? Hmmm . . . I wonder why that could be. Could it be because you didn't finish your homework?" That's when I always want to say, "Well actually lady, since you ask, it's NOT because I didn't finish my homework. It's because I didn't START it." But I never do say any such thing. I just shrug my shoulders while she goes to put another check next to my name on the chalkboard.

So all of that is bad enough, but do you want to hear what happened last week that was really awful? Okay there is this test that we have to take every year called the CAT test, which stands for California Achievement Test. This is Oregon, but for some reason we take a test from California. Anyway, Mrs. O'Connor has two bags of goodies. One of them has little things in it like peppermints, caramel chews, butterscotches, things like that. People get to pick something out of that bag for ordinary things like being a good line leader or volunteering to go get the morning milks. The other bag, however, is really special. It has good stuff in it like full-size candy bars and little puzzles. Mrs. O'Connor almost never brings that bag out but she wanted everyone to do really well on this CAT test so she said, "Whoever gets the best score on this test will get to choose something from the Big Goodie Bag." "Ooooh," everyone said. "The Big Goodie Bag."

When we took the test, I just knew I had gotten all the answers right. There wasn't any math on this test, it was just reading and writing. I couldn't wait for the scores to come back so the whole class could see that even though I stutter I'm not retarded, but am, in fact, actually lots smarter than they are. A few weeks later the scores came in and everyone wanted to know, "Who got the best score? Who is the winner?" And this is when one of the worst moments of my life occurred. Mrs. O'Connor walked over to my desk. "Chelsea Starr won. Congratulations, Chelsea," she said, and plunked a butterscotch disc down on my desk. I couldn't believe it. A butterscotch?!

Everyone knew the winner was supposed to get something out of the Big Goodie Bag. The whole class looked at me like I was a bigger piece of garbage than ever before. I wanted to say something to Mrs. O'Connor. I wanted to claim my rightful prize, but I knew I wouldn't be able to do it without stuttering really bad. So I just sat there staring at the butterscotch disc blinking my tears back and trying to swallow the big lump in my throat. Eventually the lump got so big I couldn't swallow it anymore and I had to go throw up on the wastepaper basket next to Mrs. O'Connor's desk. You can imagine how much she liked that.

Twenty dollars. T-twenty. D-dollars. Hmmm. . . . I scratch my head and feel that there is a louse underneath my fingernail. I drop it into the palm of my hand to inspect it. It's a really big one and I can see that its belly is full of blood. My blood. "I hate lice b-bugs," I say, flicking the bug onto the blacktop. I know I should buy some lice shampoo but that would eat up almost half of the money and the shampoo doesn't ever kill them all, anyway. No, I'm getting a present today, not lice shampoo.

I walk past the gyro shop next to Fred Meyer and I can hear the new song I love playing on the radio. "Walk Like an Egyptian." I go inside. The girl behind the counter is doing the dance from the video. This same girl is always working. She's so pretty and cool and her hair is humongous. If I didn't have lice I would try to copy her hairdo.

I decide to order a bagel and cream cheese. After I take a bite of my bagel I feel very thirsty. I wish I could have something to drink. Oh wait, I can—I have money! I order a pop. It's my birthday, after all.

It feels really perfect to be sitting in the gyro shop eating a bagel and drinking a pop, like a regular customer "just out for a bagel and a pop." But before I even finish my bagel, my head starts to itch really bad. Like REALLY bad. I don't want the girl to see me scratching my head in her shop. It was bad enough ordering a "P-p-p-po-po-pop," but I can't even eat because my head itches so bad. I wrap the rest of my bagel up in a napkin, take one last drink of my pop, and go outside. I go around to the side of the building and scratch and scratch. Lice bugs are under my fingernails. I feel like there are so many lice on my head that they're going to kill me, maybe. I don't want to die on my birthday so I decide that I have to buy lice shampoo today to kill at least some of these bugs. What a bummer to spend birthday money on lice shampoo. That's eight dollars. The bagel was one dollar and the pop was seventy-five cents. So that's ten twenty-five that I have left. I'm going to buy a Twix bar to share with my sister and that's a quarter, which leaves exactly ten dollars to spend on whatever I want.

I go into Fred Meyer. First to the pharmacy department to get the buying of the lice shampoo over with. It's so embarrassing. I have been buying lice shampoo from the same pharmacy worker for too long. I keep expecting him to say, "What's wrong with you, kid? Why can't you ever get rid of your nasty headlice?" But he doesn't say anything. Just puts the bottle in a bag and gives me my change.

I wander around for a little while. I look at the posters. There are three Madonna posters I want. Maybe I'll get one today but first I want to see what else there is. There is a big display of socks on sale. I think of how nice it would feel to be wearing socks right now. I got a pair of socks for

Christmas, but those are long gone. I pick out a pack of white socks. Six pairs of fold-down socks for four dollars is a good deal, right?

Six dollars left. I go look at the girls' clothes. I don't know what size I wear so I ask the lady who works there. "Well, how old are you?" she asks. "T-ten," I say. "I'm t-ten today." "Well, you're kind of small," she says. "I guess you'd probably take an eight. Look on this rack. This is the sale rack." Even on sale, most of the clothes cost more than six dollars and I start to feel bad, like I shouldn't have bought the bagel or the pop or the socks. But then I find such a cute thing: a little green jumper made out of towel material, and it costs exactly six dollars! I buy the jumper and leave the store with a huge smile on my face. It's almost summertime and now I'll have an outfit to wear!

On my way home, the pavement is burning my feet through the paper-thin soles of my fake Keds so I sit down and put on a pair of the new socks. Ooh, they feel so new and good. I walk home feeling mostly happy but also a little bit freaked out. I say a quick prayer that my mom will go out after work tonight so maybe I can be in bed by the time she gets home.

Nope. When I get home, she's already there and is as pissed off as I knew she would be. She says all the things I knew she would say, and also says how stupid it was for me to waste money on lice shampoo when she can get that for free from the welfare office. I say, "W-w-well, you never DO get it from the w-w-w-welfare office, and I'm s-s-s-sick of having headlice!" My mom hates it when you talk back to her, so now she's even madder but by some miracle the phone rings and I'm able to take that opportunity to escape from the fight without so much as a slap.

I go sit on the back porch. My sister comes out to sit with me and I can tell without asking that her money is gone. I try to cheer her up by giving her two pairs of the new socks. We eat the rest of the bagel and then just sit there wishing we had popsicles or a birthday cake or anything, really, to mark the fact that today we've been on this earth for exactly a decade. And then I remember the Twix bar! We eat it really slowly and agree that it's the most delicious Twix bar we've ever tasted. And it's one of those moments, you know? Where even though things are mostly weird and hard, you know that some things are sweet.

Squee

Gina de Vries

S quee and I almost got beat up at a bar in the Mission, but that's not what I really want to write about. What I want to write about is how she walked into Muddy Waters at Twenty-fourth and Valencia and was exactly what I needed, at least for that night. Cody and I had finally, officially, really broken up less than a week before, and Squee blustered into my life, a whirling dervish of kinky sex and primary colors and sweet talk. We ran around the Mission giggling at each other, talking politics, porn, and the friends we had in common. But it was after we narrowly avoided getting queer-bashed that we kissed. Not that the threat of violence turned us on—more that it made us want some comfort.

Squee was cute, and sweet, if a bit flighty (but what the hell should I have expected from someone who christened herself Squee?). She came to pick me up at the café for our nine o'clock date forty-five minutes late, a tall femme hurricane rushing into Muddy Waters. I looked up and I knew then that we would kiss and I grinned at her, knowing that. "Hi, are you Gina?" she said in her sweet, high voice. "Yes, and you're Squee?" "Oh, you're cute!" she said to me as I stood up, "You are too!" I was blushing, laughing. She was this tall, tall, tall—six-foot-five to my four-eleven—skinny punk transgirl, covered in leopard print and red plaid, her look a delightfully sleazy combination of call girl and schoolgirl. She had two lip piercings, these dangerous-looking spikes sticking out of either side of her labret. I found them intimidating for a second, but Squee's sweetness tempered the scariness of the metal in her mouth. I wondered what the spikes would feel like against my skin as we wandered around the Mission in search of a clean bathroom. I needed to pee very badly, and the bathroom at Muddy's was disgusting.

So many of the bars in the Mission are blasé about queer people—full of pretentious hipsters I'd never want to hang out with, but still pretty safe—that Squee and I forgot some of them aren't. We walked into this bar, and I realized a moment too late that it was one of the older neighborhood watering holes. The Mission is historically a working-class Latino and Irish neighborhood, and the bar seemed to be a holdover from the pre-gay days. An older, straight, working man's bar, full of drunk guys in flannel who stared at Squee, at Squee's short skirt on what they didn't recognize as a girl's body. *Oh fuck*, I thought, but Squee was marching ahead of me to the ladies' room, undaunted. I walked past the pool table as quickly as possible and rushed into the tiny bathroom with her.

There was a woman in the bathroom already; there was only one stall and she was in it. Squee sat on the counter and I stood next to her and we waited for the woman to finish peeing so I could pee and we could leave. Before either of us realized it, one of the men barged into the bathroom after us. He was red faced, indignant; he started yelling at Squee to leave the women's room. Squee sat behind me on the counter and I faced the man. Squee was curled up in a fetal position, she was shivering, she was so scared. She yelled back at him to leave her alone, to chill out, and he just got angrier and angrier. A drunk, livid man, storming into the women's room, to demand that one of the women leave.

Brave Gina came out somehow, and before I was even aware of it I was repeating, over and over, "She is a girl, we're both girls, we just want to use the bathroom, it's okay, she's a woman, we're both women, just let us use the bathroom, please, please. Please." He stared us down, but he left. I was thankful that I was there to protect Squee and furious at what might have happened had I not been there. Furious that I had the power to make that man listen to me, and she didn't. We knew to get out of there before the woman in the stall was through. We looked at each other and we didn't even have to say anything, we just raced through the bathroom doors as soon as the guy wasn't blocking them, past the group of men at the pool table whistling and shouting, "Was it good for you?"

I held Squee's hand as we walked to the McDonald's at Twenty-fourth and Mission, cooed to her that it would be okay, that I was sorry it had happened, that sometimes I hated the world. We kept stopping to hug. At the

McDonald's, they buzzed me into the men's toilet, because it was the only open and clean bathroom.

But I want to tell the story of what it was like to kiss Squee, how we ended up kissing in the first place. We walked down Twenty-fourth Street past Mission—were we on Shotwell? South Van Ness?—and leaned into the shadowy stairway of an underground apartment. We sat down on the cement landing, close enough to the streetlight to avoid the broken glass and syringes, close enough to the shadows to fool around and not get caught.

"Do you want to make out?" Squee asked me, blunt and utterly cheerful about it, and of course I did. I smiled, said "Okay!" and she kissed me. Her spikes didn't hurt my lips at all, but when she bit my neck they dug into my skin, left sharp little indents along with her teeth marks. Her hands were huge and warm, and she held me like I was a little doll. I kissed her face and neck, sucked on her earlobes, and she murmured to me that I was a good girl, showed me the boo-bag of sex toys she'd brought with her in case we had the time to fuck. I cursed the fact that I was staying with my parents and my mother wanted me home at midnight. I'd wanted to say, "I've been living on my own for two years, Mom," but it was the holidays and Ma was worried about me, what with the breakup and all. I felt this weird adolescent obligation to Obey My Mother; it was like staying at the house I'd grown up in magically made me sixteen again, turned me back into the obedient daughter who just wanted to make things easier for everyone else.

So Squee and I didn't fuck, because I had to be home in half an hour, but we played a sort of kinky Show-and-Tell with her bag. She had a small gas mask from the Israeli army that she said she got at a dominatrix's yard sale. My eyes went wide and I asked, "What's that for?" feeling sheepish and inexperienced—me, who liked being fucked at knife-point, but this felt way out of my league. Squee responded, casually, like she was talking about a particularly good recipe, "Ohhh, it's good for breath control and that kind of stuff. . . . " and I was impressed. *This girl is kinkier than me,* I thought. *I like that.*

Squee walked me to the BART station, decided to kneel on the floor instead of bending at the waist so she could kiss me good-bye. I stood as tall as I could; she knelt before me and leaned in, and her forehead brushed up against my nose. It was the first and only time I've ever had to lean down to kiss someone, and as her tongue slipped into my mouth I felt a momentary flutter of anxiety about every tall person I'd ever made out with: Wow, is this what it's like to be tall? You must get an awful crook in your neck making out with short people. Squee bit my lip a little and the panic subsided.

"I hear your train, girl"—she smiled at me—"and you're so damn cute that I just want to keep you here, but you'd better go." I waved to Squee through the turnstile, watched her flutter away to the exit, a bounce in her step. I skipped down the stairwell to catch my train home.

FRESHMAN YEAR

From Indestructible
By Cristy C. Road

Later in freshman year, the boys wore a disguise of disinterest, but when they opened their mouths, they asked me about metal, mechanics, and masturbation; knowing I would answer with sincerity. That year, I wasn't about being visibly feminine and I wasn't honest about wanting to kiss both girls and boys. But with each month, calling myself a girl became less of a chore, and more of a statement of self-righteous pride. I would tell myself that maybe it wasn't girls that I hated, but any conformist behavior that dismissed the anti-hero and dismissed me. I was a person without a middle class nuclear family, I wasn't curvaceous, I wasn't emotionally intact, and I wasn't that much of a heterosexual. But while I started romanticizing teenage oddities, I began feeling like a discomfited novelty towards most boys' amusement.

"When I masturbate, I totally think about boys getting it on with each other." I said in compelling honesty.

"That's awesome." Marcos responded. Marcos was into Pantera and Women.

"Do you think about boys fucking each other too?" I asked.

"Hell no, I think about stacked Puerto Rican chicks."

"Why do you gotta say chicks?" I asked. "And why do they gotta be stacked?"

"Cause chicks with little tits are nasty."

"That's fucked up, I bet you have a small dick."

In the end, I hated those boys, but at the same time, I hated myself and my ability to be just as indiscreet. One week in my first year of high school, I devoted myself to understanding what I truly want and think, as oppose to what I'm supposed to want and think. Adolescence made our

aesthetic polished and our desires tight and concise- we knew
who we wanted to be. However, every bit of influence and every
bit of society cramped on our identity and made whatever we
wanted ten times harder- its not okay to be abnormal. So, I
polished my insults and taught myself that mimicking the
slander used by those around me wouldn't make me stronger, but
just as tactless. In the argument with Marcos, I used the way
I'm socialized to see a small penis as powerless in order to
insult Marcos. So I asked myself, do I truly feel this, or am I
just aware that many males in the western world are hurt by
this? Do I really feel less of Marcos cause his penis might be
small, or because his overt sexism is challenging my experience
as a teenager? I chose the latter. I was actually terrified of
big penises.

　　We learned about the constructs that suffocated and
restricted us daily. We had questions like Why do women
compete? Why do men abuse power? Why doesn't anyone think its
normal that I masturbate? Why does the way I pee, the way I
fuck, or the way my chest looks dictate the language that's
acceptable for me to use? We aren't a malfunctioning species-
were just taught to be that way.

　　"When the penis ejaculates, the semen enters the uterus.
When semen and ovum interact, new life is created. And that's
about it for sex." said my biology teacher, during a unit on
sex education.

　　"But Mr. Rodriguez, there are more ways to have sex for
pleasure than there are ways to have sex for babies. Sex may
have some ancient definition that's just for baby making- but
its been over a thousand years. Sex is about pleasure. Cause
couples that cant make babies get it on too. We should be
learning about safe ways to have that pleasure. You know
everyone in this school bangs. Can we learn about STD
prevention instead of babies."

　　"Cristy, please save this for later- this is a sex
education Unit. The basis of sex is procreation."

"No its not. The sex youre teaching us about only talks about the pleasure of dudes. Yall know dudes gotta cum to make a baby, and girls don't. Teaching this way only feeds to the idea that a girl's pleasure isn't as important as a dudes. And hell knows everyone in this classroom wants to know how not to make babies as opposed to how to make them."

"Cristy, if you don't stop, I'm gonna ask you to leave the class."

"Awesome. The drugs are kicking in right now, anyway."

As western teenagers, we were challenged by constructs that penetrated our ill judgments. I began to unlearn my one-sided methods of shit talking while realizing how difficult it was to teach others. And while I learned how not to hate girls, but hate what TV had taught us- I knew one thing. I knew I hated the masculinity in boys, but adored it in the girls.

Part 1: Tumbleweed
Shoshana von Blanckensee

Completely by accident, we land.

I was running through the industrial part of town, my feet thudding with my heart.

I must have suddenly heard of the world, that strange afternoon.

It was quiet. It was for free.

Without myself around, it was all mine for the owning.

From Long Beach, New York, on the 80, heading west to San Francisco. In Nebraska, Bella and I pull into a gas station. I put gelatin in my Mohawk in the back of the van. I mix the gelatin with hot water from the bathroom, in an empty Coke bottle I cut in half with a pocket knife. Bella sits next to me watching, a red Popsicle dripping down the back of her hand. I am eighteen, I mean to say I'm still a boy, small hips and breasts. In a few minutes I am going to lean in and kiss her without explaining, my shirt—sour with sweat and stuck to my back. I look out into the parking lot to see if it's safe. Here in Nebraska there aren't many people, just a bunch of birds walking around, a few talking to each other in the shade.

"You gotta grow that hair out if we're gonna make any money off of you," she says. Bella's laughing a little but her face is unfolding into something. I didn't know it at the time, but she was already worth a lot of money, that gap between her teeth, those blue eyes, later in San Francisco the men would drive Bella like a Cadillac, she would make them feel so cool.

And then I press her against the carpet of the van when the birds lift in unison toward the sky. I knock some bottles and candy wrappers out of the way for her head to rest. I remember how her mouth was cherry and cold, her sticky hands wrapping around my face, careful not to mess up my hair.

Back in Long Beach, Bella's mother had kneeled in the van twenty minutes before we left and put her hands together. "Girls, this is not the right decision. You are not ready to be so far away from your families." She had tried to seem stern, taking off her sunglasses, using her fist like a mallet on the carpet. Each word separated by a heavy pause. But the desperation was just below the surface of her skin, making her eyes big and glassy. I didn't say anything because I understood her for once, all that disappointment spinning inside her. I thought of my own family on the other side of town, my mom pruning the weeds that grow along the chain-link fence that separates our yard from the next, my father trying to resuscitate the old truck in the driveway.

I had been folding laundry in the back of Rudy's Wash and Fold since I started high school, saving and saving for my escape. When I told my parents I was leaving they looked at each other quietly from where they sat, sunken into the old plaid couch. My mom said, "Okay, sweetie," and held my hand for a minute. She picked at the black nail polish on my thumb with her acrylics. "Do you want me to stay?" I asked. I felt so young. A little flutter of hurt alive in my throat. She paused, and then cocked her head to the side and pulled the corners of her mouth up into a half smile, "Nooo, sweetie."

My father stood up and stuffed his big hands into the pockets of his jeans, smiled and nodded in my direction, and then opened the front door. For a moment the afternoon light glared past him toward us, so when he shut the door behind him, everything went dark. My mother and I sat quietly as we heard the truck start and then stall in the driveway.

In the van outside Bella's house, her mom kneels on the carpet, lays her arms open, her hands facing up, and says one more time, "Please. Girls."

I look at Bella; she's twisting a piece of her long blond hair around her finger as she whines out a long "Mooooom, we're leaving, so just say good-bye."

Somewhere around Flagstaff, Arizona, Long Beach finally detaches from us, like the caboose of a train. We spend the night at a dusty little campsite called The Rancho Villa, sleeping in our blue tent, the one Bella's mom got her for Girl Scouts when she was young.

In the morning I wake up early and broiling. Our little cocoon is glowing with heat and light, the inside wet with steam. Bella and I had peeled our clothes and sleeping bags off in our sleep. She's lying on her side facing me, her mouth slightly open so I can see the tips of her front teeth, two grains of rice lined up. There is sweat beading up at her hairline, and her hand curls toward me in a gesture I recognize but don't know the meaning of. Her body is red and speckled with heat, so I unzip the side window. The tent exhales a little, and Bella's eyes open and find me. She lifts her arm toward me and presses her fingers against the letters on my naked hip. F-A-I-T-H.

I had given myself this tattoo on my sixteenth birthday— I spent that birthday alone drinking a forty and smoking pot in the back shed of my parents' house. I was reading a novel about guys in prison, which outlined the process well enough to mimic successfully. I used a lighter to heat the needle until it glowed orange and then dipped it into the ink from my mom's calligraphy set. I spent all night pricking the letters into my skin, the blood and ink mixing and staining the edge of my shirt. I was listening to the radio. *Casey Kasem's Top Forty*, humming along with the songs I recognized.

Bella runs her fingers along the letters.

"If you were going to put a word on me which one would you pick?" she asks, in a soft cracking voice, her hand taking mine and pulling me toward her. I flop onto the sleeping bag next to her and she wraps around me.

Tumbleweed. "I'd pick *tumbleweed* and put it on your belly."

Outside of our blue tent there's a little dog yapping as an RV starts its engine; here inside I'm pricking out the letters on her belly, watching the way the needle presses and then punctures the thin skin, and using a clean white sock to wipe away the blood and ink. She's got her head turned to the side and her eyes closed, every once in a while a tear sneaks out, sliding across the bridge of her nose and along the lashes of her other eye. She tells me it's not so bad if you soften your body into it, glide on the hurt like it's ice in a rink.

Tattooing Bella, I feel young and old at the same time, I mean dumb and romantic, thinking that we would be forever.

We spend all morning in the tent—pricking words into our skin. *Tumbleweed* on Bella's stomach, *Lovely* on the back of her neck, *Courage* on the top of my hand, and *Baby Boat* in between her breasts. I finish the *t* in *Boat* with Bella's hand on my shoulder, wiping the blood and ink with the sock and the damp hair on her forehead with my hand. My stomach feels achy, like an egg cracking on the side of a bowl.

"Bella, let's get married when we get to San Francisco."

She laughs. "Girls don't get married, even in San Francisco," she says, her hands on either side of my face. She is trying to kiss me and laugh at the same time, her kissing all toothy.

I remember a day in the summer between my junior and senior year when I walked over to Bella's, through the side gate, around the house to find her on the deck pinned under

Nicholas Fenton's scrawny body with her legs open. I heard her make this moan-y noise and I saw her body moving under him, her hair wet from the swimming pool, wild and crawling around her head. I yelled "Fuck you, Bella!" so loud that a dog barked on the other side of the fence and then I started running. Back around the side, through the gate and down the street toward the beach. Why did she have to fuck ugly Nicholas? I kicked the ground away harder with each step and swung my fists at my side punching at the air saying "fuck, you, fuck, you fuck, you" under my breath with each step, all the way to the boardwalk. I walked with my hands in my pockets, watching my feet on the wood planks, trying to shake this photograph I had in my brain. Then I stopped trying and leaned right up to the edge of what I had seen, Bella's thighs and the way she sounded, her two front teeth, and the space in between, her arms all the way around him and her hair, wet from the pool and messy.

A story too soft to cut.

The name of this place was the same white.

There was light before breakfast.

 I held onto the crash of us; used a nickel to decide this way or that.

A photo to prove it, in my eyes, two red suns.

Bella and I stop in Reno for the night even though we're only a few hours from San Francisco. We play some slots at Circus Circus and then get bored and find a little lezzie bar called The Blue Cactus, built like a log cabin. In a small yellow bathroom stall Bella pulls a glass vial of coke from her purse. I'm so mad for a second. "What if we got pulled over and searched!" I whisper-yell it at her. But I guess I'm over it really fast because here I am in the stall with my thumb covering my right nostril, Bella on the other side of the toilet, holding the black spoony-thing up to my left nostril.

In the stall next to us we hear a girl crying that kind of choking cry. We stop to recognize the sound and then we make big faces at each other. Faces that say, "Oh no, poor her" and "She's depressing me." I wipe the outside of Bella's nose with the sleeve of my shirt and she laughs and then covers her mouth dramatically. The girl thinks we're laughing at her, and I know it. I grab Bella's hand and unlock the stall door, drag her out into the bar as fast as we can, because really I don't want to see her or hear her anymore, the crying girl I mean. Like watching a bird getting eaten by a cat. Something about little eyes, body in a vice grip. I don't even turn when I hear the bathroom door open and then swing shut behind us a few moments later. I've got a perfect shot into the left corner, my vision is crisp on the pool table and just beyond where things begin to distort and fuzz, Bella's hand rests on her belt buckle. Not in my own voice, I say something, but I can't really hear what I say. Bella and I are laughing, the ash from her cigarette dropping onto the green felt of the table.

Back in Long Beach when I am four I fall off my board while I'm surfing on the rocking chair. I tumble in the waves so my heart crackles and I try to find up, but instead I smash my head open on the stone fireplace. My sweatpants are green; I sit up and watch a little spill of blood dribble onto them, blue spots, blue blops. A noise comes out of my mouth but I don't make it. My dad runs in and lifts me by my arms, so my head swings back. My eyes find the ceiling and our shadow, cast across it by the lamp on the end table. My fingers are splayed, long and extending across to the far wall. "Get the truck!" he hollers to my mom and somewhere there is the sound of keys.

My eight-year-old sister leans in the doorway wearing one of my dad's T-shirts, the armpits stained yellow. She's holding a hard-boiled egg, in the other hand a pile of shells, her hair tousled and her toenails painted red. Our eyes press right into each other, like a walkie-talkie made from string and tin cans.

Talking to my head wound instead of me, my father leans in and yells "Goddamn it" at it a couple of times. My cat Nilla watches from the window as I'm carried out to the driveway.

In the truck we sit on a shower curtain because the roof leaked in winter and the seats rotted out, old broccoli in a plastic bag, grosser than gross. My father takes off his shirt and wraps it around my head so tight it pulls my eyes off to one side. His chest covered in brown hair, he smells like Irish Spring and I'm resting against him. I can see out the top of the windshield, the telephone wires dipping and swinging back up into blue; occasionally a bird nicks the line, but I go crazy right around this part. The memory of that drive to the hospital suddenly explodes, scattering in all directions. The sounds of his mouth following behind every opening.

* * *

A couple days after I caught Nicholas Fenton moving on Bella like she was a rocking horse I thought, "If Bella could, could want to I mean, then I could, too."

That afternoon, wild with salty winds blowing in from the Atlantic, I was by myself, boycotting Bella, putting my headphones on when she tried to talk to me. I flung my backpack in a circle for a few blocks, swinging at everything, and the streets were crying too. *Fucking Fenton* his head would roll. Believe me, I felt crazy enough. I tumbled this way, out toward the beach, the sound of seagulls and the wind burning, sending a couple tears horizontal into my hair. I found Todd out by the arcade on the boardwalk and dragged him by his wrist down the stairs into the sand and then underneath into the cold.

I would pull up this afternoon, tear it out from the rest, pull up my T-shirt to show him. Lay back so I could feel the sand in my hair. It was an introduction, revenge, and a conclusion, the only guy I was ever with. I remember the smell of damp wood, damp tobacco from old cigarette butts, and long splinters of light pressing through the slats, the way he took off his jacket said *Can you handle all this?* There was sweat on his neck to the left of me and to the right, wide open, white beach, the water and the sky—one giant expanse of blue, my pants tying my ankles together and Todd saying stupid things he probably heard in a porn somewhere.

Could I do this again and again? Find a way to belong right here?

I went home quieter, my mind reeling, my mom knocking on the bathroom door saying, *get out of the shower and set the table.* I sat in my bed wrapped in a towel, my hair dripping down my face, my brain spinning around and around. My room was small and talking too, saying things like *Who are you? You can get out of here,* and *Fat chance weirdo.* I flopped back and closed my eyes. Something is all wrong. A little tremor rising, not because of what I'd done with Todd underneath the boardwalk, but a tremor projected out in time in front of me. Wondering what this life will feel like. What will it be like now that I'm sure.

And this was my first sight: floors and bed, greasy and so on.
    At dusk the hallway to the front door—slunk out a sound.
    The street pointing which direction to take.
    The glow of each streetlight appearing closer together in the distance, as if picking up speed, taking off in flight.

In San Francisco a year or so after we arrive, we are twenty I think, Bella and I. Bella finally got us jobs dancing at the Chez Paree, after nine months of folding laundry at the Wash and Fold across from the residential hotel on Ellis Street. My hair is to my shoulders like a regular lady, and she was right, we would make some money off of me.

All the girls who work at the Chez Paree call it the cheese parade when the manager isn't around. He takes everything real personal, like we're calling him a cheese parade. Angela goes right up to a sailor and says, "Welcome to the cheese parade, can I take your order please?" The girls in the dressing room laugh and laugh, like trying to outlaugh each other when it really isn't that funny.

In the dressing room Doni squeezes milk out of her boobs

into the trash before she goes on stage, or else she leaks, and my favorite girl is Angela, really short with no boobs. She spends all her stripping money at the circus school. She can slither backward up the pole. I stop watching her do it after Doni tells her I'm a big "gay rod." I don't know how to respond to being called gay rod. So I laugh with my eyebrows squinched together and lifted a little. I don't like Angela in the "gay rod" way, but more important, I don't want her to think I like her. Someone tells me she's super Christian and thinks everything is a sin.

We're in the dressing room and Bella takes our picture with a disposable camera; the flash leaves two suns, one in each eye. Bella puts the camera down, sits in a metal folding chair, and looks at her teeth in the mirror. They're white and square. It seems like a hundred years ago in our blue tent, my kiss landed on her two front teeth by accident, like Chiclets I thought, and I didn't mind kissing them.

She's looking in the mirror, picking at her front teeth with her pinky. Girls hate her because she gives hand jobs. I knew she would. I feel mad, so I can't look her in the eye like I used to. Doni calls her a slut, and I tell her not to judge. Then Doni spreads a rumor that I give hand jobs. I laugh really loud every time I hear it. I laugh one big "Ha," a "Ha" that sounds more like a cough than a laugh. I have never given a hand job in my entire life. I wouldn't know how if I wanted to. Secretly it hurts my feelings. Doni and I are friends. Sometimes I take care of her baby, Jackson, a fat little one-year-old, while Doni is working at the club. Jackson and I lay in Doni's bed at night watching *Sesame Street* videos. He holds onto one of my fingers as he falls asleep, his pacifier bobbing quietly in his mouth, smelling clean and milky and completely new.

Doni wants Jackson to go to the Montessori school and then Harvard or Yale. I tell her I think he will, because I can see her desire so close to the surface, rumbling right underneath her skin.

In Long Beach, New York, 1986, my sister and I walk by ourselves to the beach in flip-flops and big round sunglasses. I'd just turned twelve and I'm wearing a new jean skirt over my swimsuit. This is mid-June, when Long Beach smells like salt and sweat. The air is wet, dense, just around noon I think. I have quarters for an Italian ice, metallic in my hand; I do a little dance in my pocket so I jingle, jingle, jingle. I am thinking about amphibians. The bullfrogs in my grandma's yard are leaping in the bushes; I'm trying to catch the little monsters. My grandma's dog killed one a couple weeks ago. I told my sister it looked like someone had dropped a turkey potpie in the driveway. Their insides are gray and later I want to ask my dad why.

My sister pulls me by the arm, so I look up and the street comes into bright focus, past a man walking toward us; he has gray eyes. He leans into me as we pass and whispers something that I can't understand, but his breath is peculiar, the way it coils up and slides into my ear. The smell of him is salty and reddish or yellow as I turn to watch him pass, his hands in his pockets, the buildings swaying around and a few cars driving by without realizing. Later at the beach I take my skirt off and sit in my bathing suit with a coconut Italian Ice in my hand. My sister is collecting cigarette butts next to me and making a design with them in the sand. I can't stop thinking about the man on the street. He likes me. He likes me. He likes me.

We have this kind of power, a little chipped around the edges.
The eyes get round when we push our legs into focus.
Someone whispers, "Oh, you're good. You're not too good. You're good enough for me." This is how the war begins, on any given afternoon.
A body—a whole country, so eager to explode.

Chris walks into the Chez Paree while I'm on stage completely naked laying on my back, propped up a little on my elbows, swinging my legs open and closed in big sweeping flops, so my pussy goes from an I to a capital A and back again. When I do this I feel silly but it's really time consuming when you've got a long slow song—besides, no one ever complains. I am dancing to that terrible song, "Wicked Game," and I can see Bella sitting at a table in the back eating mashed potatoes from a styrofoam bowl. In between bites she lip-synchs along like she really likes it a lot. Chris sits in a chair right next to the stage, only I don't know she's Chris yet. She's just this woman, kind of butch but with really manicured eyebrows. I smile at her and wink while she folds a twenty and puts it next to my foot, a piece of her fuzzy blond hair dropping between her big fish eyes.

When the song ends I pull back the red curtain and run

down the carpeted ramp into the dressing room. "She's mine," I tell the girls, even though they already know. I have dibs on any woman that comes in here, just because I like them better. Same as Angela has dibs on sailors. I walk straight out of the dressing room and as I approach her, she stands up, gesturing toward the back of the club. I turn and she follows me, back toward the red-curtained booths.

A week later I agree to meet Chris at the bar on the corner, an East Coast–style sports bar misplaced in San Francisco. Chris doesn't know it but we are here to negotiate.

I pull a stool up next to her, she buys me a gin and tonic, and I thank her in a voice higher than my own so it ends up sounding almost like "Tank you." I have chosen an outfit to accompany my new profession, a red skirt with a slit up the side and the smallest and lowest cut shirt I own, black and cinched up the front, so I have to keep checking to see if one of my boobs hasn't accidentally popped out.

"I want 1,200 dollars for a twelve-hour night, at least seven of those hours taken up with sleeping, and no more than two hours of sex." I say it like a speech directed at the ice in my drink, which I poke with a tiny red straw. I say it like a speech, just like I'd planned it lying in bed at the residential hotel, next to Bella who was sleeping with her arms over her head. My eyes were open toward the bluish cast of headlights that slanted and faded across the ceiling, my mouth wrapping silently around the shape of each word.

Chris doesn't hesitate. She reaches into her pocket and says, "Do you want me to pay you now?"

Stupid. Cocky. I do a little giggle and take a little sip.
A good plan. A month away from the club. Easy.

Chris is incredibly weird looking, like a ham and melon
snack with a toothpick holding it together, but then add this
big flop of fuzzy blond blow-dried hair. I guess I mean her
face doesn't make any sense, her features barely holding
together

She's one of the top engineers of the Department of Public
Transportation and makes so much money it's sick. In a loft
south of Market she spends a lot of time listening to the
radio, pulling the panties off of various girls with her teeth so
maybe they will fall in love with her. A line or two, or a
couple Vicodin, and mornings standing in the shower for a
good hour letting the water pour over her eyes, breathing
slow through her mouth.

I only know because I caught her once. It was the
morning after my last night with her. The door to the bathroom was open so I snuck in to see her, slightly warped by
the clear shower curtain, the water turning her into a pasty
impressionist painting. Her arms at her side and her hair
wet and slick, covering half of her face. The skylight was
doing something strange to the light and the morning,
drawing me toward her, pulling my stomach into my chest,
so I had to turn and leave out the front door without saying
good-bye. The big roll of cash she had put in one of my
shoes when she woke up, now held tight in my fist, planted
firmly in my jacket pocket. I was passing nobody on the
street for a good mile on my way home, believing that it

was a sign of something, a flock of birds swooping in unison and then splashing every direction across the blue.

But the first time—

I'm lying on the floor of her loft too stoned. Really it might be a dream or someone else's life. If I open my mouth to speak I will probably tell her something true so I have to keep my mouth closed, don't slip out on accident.

"Chris, come here and fuck me." Not because I have to, but because I'm bored of the way my body feels.

She moves from the couch to meet me on the floor wrapping her arm around me more gently than I would have expected. She's not my type and her skin is hot and smells like someone I don't know. These are my hips tilting toward hers, but she could be anybody, and now my vision cuts up into bite-size pieces and my skin creaks and splinters off, floating downstream. I see her face only in pieces, one eye, an ear, and the weight of her on top of me. I kiss her as sweet as I can, with my mouth that is attached to no part of me, my arms wrapping around her back, one holding the other at the wrist.

A couple hours later we're sitting on the couch watching a *90210* rerun on channel 20; I can feel Chris looking at me but I don't turn toward her. Her hand slides along my arm and curls around my thumb. I glance at her as I pull myself out of her grip. "Are you trying to hold my hand?" I ask. I feel disgusted and I don't know why. A little wave of hurt washes over her face but she laughs, and it slips away.

"You can fuck for money but you won't hold my hand?"

I can feel the heat rising in my cheeks but I turn back to

the TV and the burning starts to dissipate. Dylan's father just exploded on his yacht. I saw this episode when it first came out. Bella and I were high and eating donut holes on her parents' white couch, a Wednesday night, our senior year.

How many people can we be?

I came home, my mouth wet, so I pushed cake inside of it.

After I ate I held someone's hand under the table, it was cold, it was mine.

Still I'd do it all over again.

To learn ourselves so gradually, when we never meant to.

When we don't believe in life it will be terrifying, I mean, so necessary.

Bella says she won't be friends with me if I whore for Chris. We are sitting on the roof of our building in aluminum lawn chairs in our underwear and T-shirts. My knees are up so I can pinch Potrero Hill between them if I close one eye. "Whoring is different then hand jobs," she explains. I don't look at her when she says it. I'm framing a blue water tower between my knees and thinking about the letters we had dug into each other. *Courage*—a faded gray scrawling on the top of my hand.

"Whatever," I say quietly, as I get up and pull my pants on. I leave Bella on the roof, circle down the staircase, and swing the door open that leads out onto Ellis Street. I start walking fast toward nowhere, my arms crossed over my chest.

I don't believe her. I don't believe her but she's right. She won't say another word to me for six years, until we meet again accidentally, her face much softer and full; we will grasp onto each other and start giggling in disbelief.

My name is caught with a fishhook, pulled jerking from my mouth.

Alone I am a continent with big teeth.

This California—a language I don't speak, the lonely clank of stucco.

What I wanted to say but couldn't, to have Bella for keeps.

I was dumbstruck.

When I opened my mouth, my mouth said, "   ."

A couple days after my first night with Chris I'm walking down by Third Street and all the industrial buildings. I've got a big sweatshirt on and jeans and no makeup and my hair is pulled back under a beanie because this way I can pass as a man if you don't look too close at my face. I'm exploring an old building debating whether I should climb the metal stairs inside up to some kind of weird machinery, when I smell a terrible smell and turn in circles looking to see where it's coming from. Behind the stairs I see feet sticking out and as I peer under I can tell the guy is dead from the position of his body. Like he got twisted and tossed there and after I see his gray putty face I just start running. I run out of the building out into the street and toward the water. My chest is heaving right out of me, but not because I'm scared, but out of that strange electricity I haven't felt since I was a kid. Running, my body just like a train because it feels crazy and I can. I pass nobody on the street and leap over a newspaper floating up on a cold wind. My brain says, "Nobody, nobody, nobody, nobody," over and over again, but I don't know who it's referring to.

Bella moved out in November of that second year in San Francisco, that year the Bay Area had a cold front that wouldn't pass. It felt like Long Beach when I was a kid, my breath fogging in front of me, perched on the moment between fall and winter.

On Thanksgiving morning I wake up alone in the hotel on Ellis Street. Out the window I can see a line forming outside of Saint Mary's Charitable Services. I sit up in bed and peer out, wondering if I should go down and get in line. Not because I can't afford food, but because I have a brick forming, square in the middle of my chest, so lonely and strange. I try and force it down for a good half hour. Outside a lady is wearing a green sweatshirt with a puffy turkey on it. She gets in line and starts laughing with the guy in front of her.

I could call my family. I could call Doni or Angela. I could even call Bella.

- Hello?
- Chris?
- Ya?
- Hi, it's Scarlet.
- Well Happy Thanksgiving, Scarlet.
- Hey I was wondering if you wanted to change our Saturday date to tonight, because Saturday's not looking too good.

- Honey you know I want to but it's Thanksgiving. I'm picking my brother up in a few hours.
- That's ok, I was just asking.
- You want to see me, don't you?
- Chris. Didn't anyone ever tell you? Don't bet your heart on a working girl.
- You sound like a country song, Scarlet.
- I am a country song, Chris.
- Ok I gotta go. We'll just keep it on Saturday.
- That's ok?
- Ya, I just had to do something but I can do it another day. So I'll see you then.
- Good. Can't wait. Bye, Chris.
- Bye, Scarlet.

I hang up the phone and sit there staring at the line forming in the street below, the turkey sweatshirt lady and her new friend, a guy with an American flag baseball hat. I light one of Bella's half-smoked cigarettes I find in the ashtray mug on the floor, take a drag, and then put it out.

I lift slowly from the top of my head toward the ceiling and then out of the room—where I expand into something the size of a small planet, but less solid. Soft like a cloud. I pick the room up in my hands, as if the ceiling were made of glass, and it was really a diorama of a room with a girl sitting up in bed naked. She has ratty black hair, her knees pulled against her chest, her face turned toward the window so the morning light falls into her eyes which are brownish green, set far apart on her face. A bluish cast, like the faintest bruise under each eye. Her ribs are visible on her back, forming two ladders on either side of her spine. The sheets are dark flannel so you can't tell they haven't been washed recently. There are clothes strewn all over the floor, and in one corner is a sink and a counter with a hot plate on it, in the other, a dresser and in the bottom drawer a sock filled with one hundred dollar bills.

The girl in the room stands up and squats over a mason jar on the floor. She pees and then pours the pee into the sink and rinses the jar out. She begins to sort through the clothes. Her body makes me cringe. Her pussy—shaved with a slight razor rash redness to it. Knobby knees. She finds a pair of tube socks with green and yellow stripes, a pair of underwear she turns inside out and pulls on. Black jeans. An oversized black hooded sweatshirt she pulls on with nothing underneath, then a beanie and a jean jacket and a down vest over it and red skiing gloves.

She grabs her keys and opens the door on the side of the box, stepping out and shaking in the cold—the shaking bringing me back. I'm walking down the hallway of the hotel and I begin to feel my legs again. How I can move them underneath me. I tell them what to do, and then they do what I say. I experiment with my arms, too. I tell them to swing and flap and then they swing and flap.

Money

Jenny Lowery

I pick up the phone to order Chinese food from down the street and instead of a dial tone I hear a slow click-click-click. I sigh and return the receiver to the cradle. The phone bill didn't get paid again this month. I flop down on the couch and start putting on my shoes. I knew the bill was late, but I guess we're a little beyond late. I grab my sweater off the hook by the door and start walking down the street toward Chang's Chinese Palace. The air is chilly and sharp. The heat from the evening sun doesn't make it to my shoulders before losing its warmth. It's late October but the leaves are still fully green. Almost like they're teasing me into believing the sun will stay around forever. Three people should be able to pay the bills on one rented apartment. Why can't we keep our heads above water? I work full time and Kevin is getting steady unemployment. Maddy lives the artist's lifestyle but she always seems to come through when the rent is due. I have a suspicion that it's her father who buys her paintings. Maybe I can make him a clay ashtray and he'll pay our phone bill.

Chang's is packed. School is back in session and the students from the state college one block over favor this establishment. Probably for the same reasons I do. Cheap and close. The air is thick and oily and feels tangibly wet. The windows are steamed over and a little girl writes her name in the fog. She is wearing dinosaur pajamas and a tiara. The food her mother has ordered is ready and the girl gets packed back into her coat and ushered out the door, the food swinging from the crook of her mother's finger. Little boxes wrapped in plastic bags. I order and push my way back outside. The crispness of the air brings a burn to my throat like I've been running.

Two young males lean against the wall of the restaurant talking. I pick a spot and lean against the wall several feet from them. They look the frat boy type. Overpriced T-shirts, excessive volume, three-dollar words used out of context. The conversation turns to Internet porn. I wonder what their parents think all that expensive electronic equipment padding out the Visa bill is used for. Junior isn't studying with it.

"Dude, Tiffany just got a check for six hundred bucks for writing a story that got published in *Playgirl*. I haven't seen the article or anything cuz that mag's kinda gross. Gay."

"Who's Tiffany?"

"This girl I'm going out with. English major. She's pretty hot."

Did he say six hundred dollars for a trashy romance story? I mean, for *Playgirl* doesn't it have to be a trashy romance story? I can write that crap. My sisters and I use to write stuff like that all the time on road trips. We had to do something while we were crammed into the back of a Volvo station wagon headed for Yellowstone. We would all write a paragraph and then trade papers. Each of us would add a second paragraph and trade again, trying to outdo each other in absurdity. Our mother had asked us once what we were writing about. Amber, the quick-witted one among us, said fairies.

"Oh, isn't that lovely, dear?" Mother says, poking my father in the arm. The three of us doubled over with giggles.

Mom had a huge collection of cookie-cutter romance novels she read in the bathtub. We borrowed several of these books without her knowledge and read them in the under-the-covers-with-a-flashlight style. We followed the same predictable pattern as these novels in our little stories, flirting with words like *bulge* and *blossoming womanhood*.

When each of us turned thirteen we got The Talk. I had already heard The Talk twice before from my sisters, plus the stuff they had learned on the playground at school. So when it was my turn I was more excited about getting to be the center of attention when I went back to give my report on what she said than I was about getting the info in the first place.

My mother surprised all three of us that day. The Talk I got was different than my sisters. We don't know why exactly. Maybe she knew that by telling one, the others would hear it, too. Maybe she thought I was The Romantic of her offspring and needed the emotions of sex as well as the mechanics. Maybe she had just read a new parenting book. She had definitely read too many of her novels, because I remember vividly her description of an orgasm and how it was like hearing *Ode to Joy*. I still blush when I think of relaying that scene to Amber and Jill. Stammering through it with red ears and sweaty palms. What a waste of center stage.

Chang's door opens and I hear a grunt.

"Sweet and Sour chicken? I've been calling your name. Food's ready."

I grab my little boxes tucked into a plastic bag and start for home. Mid-block I turn around and head the other direction. Around the corner is a gas station. Behind the counter, to the left of the cigarettes, is a wide selection of brown paper-wrapped magazines. I ask the clerk for a *Playgirl*. A small smirk plays at the corner of his mouth.

"I'm sorry, miss. What did you say? I couldn't hear you."

Jackass. I repeat my request and he rings me up. I do not put my pennies in the little blue saucer on the counter.

I crawl into bed with a fork and a notepad as soon as I hit the door. I thumb through my new purchase trying not to look at the pictures. Muscle men dripping in oil and fake tans are just not my thing. Kevin will be happy to recycle it for me, though. Maybe I can use it as incentive to get him to clean the kitchen. Or take that couch he found by the neighbors' dumpster back down where it came from. It smells like a small animal died in it. And he watches Martha Stewart every day so he should know that plaid does not go with our décor, struggling chic.

I find what I'm looking for. In small print toward the back, after the advertisements but before the classifieds I find the call for submissions. Erotic stories, original, yadda yadda, one dollar per word. One dollar per word! I could easily write a one thousand word piece. I begin to write furiously. I do not stop. I do not edit. I do not grab my thesaurus. I am practiced at this writing style. I need to thank my sisters.

Maddy knocks on my door and peeks her paint-flecked head in. I have no idea how much time has passed. She gives a curious glance to my notebook. Her overalls are unsnapped and hanging around her waist.

"More poetry?"

"No, something a little different. What's up?"

"Um, did you know the phone has been shut off again?" She looks distraught.

"Yep."

"Can I read what you're writing?"

I hand her the notebook.

I slowly rolled the orchid between my thumb and forefinger. The fragrance of the flower beds from which I just plucked this beauty filled the late-afternoon air. It's not my nature to laze, scantily clad, by the poolside gazing at orchids but I had a purpose. Mario, my new pool boy, was expected today. It would be his first time cleaning my pool, so I allowed myself to believe that I needed to stick around and watch. Just to make sure he did a good job. His chocolate eyes and mocha skin had nothing to do with it. Nor did his snug Levis or that succulent bulge he was hiding beneath them.

Maddy was blushing.

"I thought you were a dyke."

"I'm just trying to pay the phone bill."

Tail of a Bondage Model

Tina Butcher

I couldn't keep anything down. Not since early two mornings previous when I had started my seventeen days of travel through the European bondage circuit. I had worked as a traveling bondage model for the past couple years, shooting in the States, but this was my first venture to Europe. My travels hadn't started off so well, with me curled up in the fetal position and shivering on the airplane for twelve hours while my stomach twisted and turned. But regardless of minor bumps in the road or in the air, I did love my job. It paid well and allowed me to be kinky, creative, and support my own artistic endeavors in San Francisco as a writer. I had it made. I led my life as both Tina Butcher the writer and activist and Madison Young the kinky girl next door. I was seeing far-off lands, meeting new people, and getting material to write about. Although this life seemed all peaches and crème, it did come with the occasional vomitus spew from reality.

For instance, the erratic and intense traveling schedule had been one of the many cracks in the foundation of my most recent relationship, leading to our final breakup. When I first started to travel for work I told her that my biggest fear was that one day I would leave and come back and she would be gone. She promised me that this would never happen, but that was before having to deal with two years of living with a bondage model.

I was headed from London to Copenhagen and then back to London. I made all my travel arrangements last minute so I was forced to take the train through Brussels, Germany, and finally to Denmark. My perception of time was completely distorted. I would wake up in a different airport or train station or country, eat something, get violently sick, wait around the station for a couple hours, get sick again, and board the train to the next city. I'd torn a big hole in my stomach from the sudden drinking binges that had resulted from the recent breakup between me and my now ex-girlfriend, Gauge. She had left my insides black and blue, and I felt that if I jumped on enough trains I might be able to escape the thought of her.

I hadn't eaten a good meal in days. The stations, planes, and trains offered very little I could eat on my vegan diet. I finally found an Asian Fusion restaurant in Germany and decided to take my chances. I ordered veggie chow mein, fumbled in my pocket to find the correct bills for the country I was in, paid the snarling tourist-hating clerk five Euros, and sat down with my food. "I hate tourists, too," I wanted to say. I wanted to let her know that I wasn't one of them. That I was a working-lower-class gal from the States who had just

gotten thrown into this whole mess. I wasn't here with
Mommy and Daddy's gold card.

I sat down and started shoveling food into my mouth with
the wooden chopsticks. I was starving. I felt like I hadn't
eaten in days and technically I think that I was right but I
couldn't quite tell due to the time difference. The cheap
crunchy vegetables snapped under my teeth and I slurped up
thin noodles that I twirled around the chopsticks. The vegetables were so cheap they had little nutritional value. They
had thrown in mostly bamboo, onion, garlic, and pepper. But
I was so hungry I lapped up half the plate and felt like that
was all I could manage. My stomach was shrinking from
eating so little and I couldn't handle a full plate of food yet.
I placed my dish in the dish bin and headed out into the mad-
ness of the station. Neon and fluorescent lights everywhere.
People in swarms rushing through tunnels and passages,
being pushed to the surface like worms after the rain. I made
my way aggressively through the crowd to the bookstore.

I stopped at the information desk. "'Scuse me, miss. Do
you know if there is any place in the station with Internet or
where I could plug in my laptop?" The young woman at the
informed me, in a thick German accent, that I needed to go
to the Internet café a block from the station.

I exited the station doors and made my way into the city
streets of Kolon, Germany. The air was nice and brisk. Not
even as cold as San Francisco evenings. It circulated its way
through my nostrils and air passages filtering out all the stale
train air I'd been breathing.

I turned the corner and found the Internet café. The cute German girl who worked there pointed to a computer in the back of the café and I attempted to log on with the foreign keyboard made of an unfamiliar order of letters and punctuation. The connection was deadly slow and I couldn't even get my messages to load. My fingers struggled to find the words on the keyboard, but the keys' chaotic order gave my fingertips a desperate stutter, and the slow connection left me with snapped vocal chords. I fiddled around with it another couple of minutes, and then it hit me. My insides cramped violently in spasms of revolt from my veggie chow mein. I ran to the front of the café.

"Do you happen to have a bathroom I could use?"

"Down the hall," she said.

I bolted down the long hallway as my guts continued to spasm. I ran into the toilet and dropped my pants. The first explosion didn't make it into the toilet. I splattered half on the floor and half on my panties. The heap of toxic blackness that sprung forth from my body was unlike anything I'd ever seen before. I slid my way onto the porcelain receptacle, clinging to the basin like a lover. My body exploded again and again, producing more and more liquified black shit for my smooth white porcelain friend who spooned my weak and infantile body with a comforting coolness.

I stayed in the toilet a good fifteen minutes, letting out everything toxic until I felt that I could move again. I looked up from my seat for the toilet paper. There was none. I looked at the sink. There was no soap either. The room was equipped with a roll of paper towels which I used to wipe up my ass, the floor, the crap off my shoes, the crap off my undies, and anywhere else that I found crap. Unfortunately they didn't have a garbage can in the bathroom, either. I had to leave the crap-saturated towels in the corner behind the toilet. I thought about flushing them but there were too many, and the last thing I needed was to flood the café. I rinsed my hands. I smelled disgusting. I felt disgusting. I hadn't showered in three days, and I still had a twelve-hour train ride ahead of me.

Night and day flashed before me on the train to Copenhagen. I got ill a couple of times on the train, but it wasn't too bad. I kept sipping on the water that I had gotten at the Asian Fusion restaurant, trying to keep hydrated. I felt good enough to read some Bukowski for part of the ride and to work on an article I had due that week for a queer lifestyle magazine. I was writing an article for their travel section on a burlesque troupe I had seen in Seattle. The editor needed a last-minute piece and since she knew I was constantly traveling, she figured I'd have something to write about. I fell asleep with my neck leaning awkwardly against the train window. This had been my sleeping position for far too long, leaving my neck in bad shape. During bondage trips, the traveling was the hardest part for my body. Sleeping slouched in a little ball on the train, bus, or plane with my neck crooked off to one side for hours of travel was chronically painful. I needed a massage. Officers boarded the train and asked for my passport. I was half-asleep and shuffled though my pack for my passport. I finally found it.

"Hmmm . . . Tina Marie, huh? Did you know that your name is Danish?"

"Really? I didn't know that."

I wasn't impressed. I didn't care. My mother had chosen my name from an actress on a TV show and if I hadn't been Tina it would have been Olivia after Olivia Newton John. I felt like the origin of my name came more directly from pop culture than Denmark.

I arrived in Copenhagen and needed to decide on a plan of action. I had the address for the hotel that Katrina, the Danish bondage producer, had booked for me, and the name my room was reserved under Madison Young. I hadn't been able to reach Katrina by phone, largely due to my dead cell phone and my recharger's incapability with European electrical outlets. But I was exhausted and figured that if I could make it through four different countries to get to Copenhagen then I could manage checking into the hotel without assistance. I would try to call Katrina again after I had rested and bathed.

I was sick of buses and trains, so I looked for a cab. There were dozens of them in front of the train station. I grabbed one.

"I need to go to the Grand Hotel, please."

"Oh, miss, that is right around the corner. Just turn left at the light."

I almost didn't feel like I could manage to make it that far. But I also knew it was ridiculous to take a cab, so I rolled my suitcase around the block and through the doors of the

Grand Hotel. It was a charming place. Cherry wood molding grew up the walls like vines, and the lobby was lit by delicate crystal chandeliers that branched from the ceiling. I looked like shit. I probably smelled like it, too.

"Hi, I'm checking in under a reservation for—Madison Young."

"Oh yes! Well, Miss Young, we have you down for a reservation, but it is for tomorrow night."

"Ummm, well can I switch it? I need a place to stay tonight."

"Let's see what we have available. Yes. I think we can get something for you."

"Also you see I need um . . . an adapter? My cell phone won't charge in your outlets."

"I understand. Here you are, miss. And your key. You will be staying in room five-fifteen."

"Thank you."

I really liked this hotel. Finally I would find a bed and be able to charge my phone and take a bath. Oh, yes, a long hot bath!

I took the elevator to my room. I threw my bags down and went to the bathroom to run a nice hot bath, but there was no bath; only a sink, toilet, and showerhead that jutted from the wall. There wasn't even a shower. The shower area was level with the toilet and sink. There was a shower curtain at least, but it didn't really do anything, as the water went wherever it wanted.

I stripped my clothes off. Disgusting. I felt ill about my hygiene. How had they even let me check in? The front desk man mentioned that I looked tired, but that was all. I looked more than tired. My hair was dirty and oily. I had dark circles forming under my eyes, my breath was hellacious, my lips were chapped, my clothes were soiled and my pants gravitated closer to the ground with every step. I was weak and ill and, yes, tired. It was kind to say that I looked tired. The warm water hit my body and I nearly orgasmed, it felt so fucking good. The water ran through my hair, into my eyes, my mouth, down my breasts, down my arms, running past my pussy, down my legs, puddling at my feet. I leaned against the tile. I'm sure much fucking had happened pressed against that tile wall, but I didn't need to think about that right now. Clean thoughts, clean thoughts. I lathered up my body washing my pits, pussy, feet and breasts lingering longer than necessary in all the right places. I brushed my teeth, my gums bled. I spit blood into the showery floor. I turned the water off. Dried in one of the nice fluffy white towels and collapsed on the big white down comforter. It was so soft. I just rolled around on it and curled under the sheets. I held the comforter close to my body and pretended that I still had my Gauge, that I could still feel her soft skin, put my hands on her warm perky breasts, dig my fingers through her tangled mess of pubic hair and into her wet cunt that always seemed to be ready for me. God how I loved that woman when she let me in, when she let down her guard. I loved her always, but I really loved her when her legs were wrapped around me. When she needed me to be close. When we were outside of the bed, she thought about the others. The others that I wrote about, the others that I had dinner with and talked to and who sometimes I wanted to fuck. And I had sinned because I wanted those things. I lost her. She had left while I was gone. Does that make sense? Can someone leave another person if they are already gone? I loved her. I trusted her and I think that she did the same with me. To an extent. But she always had her eye on the door, and it made her uneasy.

My body was exhausted and ready for sleep but my mind had run off to Gauge and caused my cunt to ache. Damn that hungry cunt. It would keep me from sleep until I fed it. I grabbed my Hitachi magic wand out of my backpack full of necessities, shoes and dental dams spilling out from the over-stuffed bag. The Hitachi and its cord arduously made its way out of the pile of never-ending crap. I plugged the Hitachi into the European converter and into the electrical outlet. My hand had started rubbing at my cunt already and I was getting wet and excited. I could feel my Gauge nestled up against me rubbing her wet cunt up against mine. I missed feeling her soft wetness up against me. My fingers dug into my moist mound and I pressed the Hitachi up against my clit as I flipped the switch.

Fuck!

A jolt of electricity shocked my covetous body and the lights went out along with the electric vibe. Ummm . . . was that me? Did I do that? Did my Hitachi just cause a power outage? Shit. I got up and put on some clean pants and peaked out my door. The hotel guests meandered outside of their rooms in darkness, confused and in a mild state of panic. Not only had I blown my electricity but the entire hotel's. Fuck. All I wanted to do was get off and get some sleep and now this. I decided little was to be done. The management would fix the situation and soon all the spoiled hotel guests would have their power back and be able to watch their MTV. I unplugged my fried Hitachi and placed her back in my backpack. She had had a nice run of things. Gauge and I had fucked a lot with that vibrating vixen and she had made Gauge ejaculate for the very first time. But I supposed that it was fitting that she go up in smoke only a week after the demise of our couple-dom. My eyes got heavy and I passed out naked, wet, and holding the memory of Gauge close and staring at the deceased Hitachi which peeked its head from my bag.

I woke up to the phone ringing. I jumped up and answered.

"Hello?"

"Madison? It's Katrina."

"Oh my God! It is so good to hear from you. I've been trying to get a hold of you and I couldn't get into my voice mail and my phone was dead and oh God it is good to hear from you. So . . . I'm at the hotel and I figured I could just stay with you tomorrow night if that is ok?"

"Sure. Sure. That won't be a problem. I got your e-mail mentioning your arrival but I mixed up the dates. I also saw that you're vegetarian so I'll make sure to have some food around the house that you can eat."

"Oh that is so sweet. Thanks, Katrina."

"Sure. Sure. I'll pick you up tomorrow morning at the hotel at 9:30. Does that sound good?"

"Sounds great."

"See you then. Cheers."

"Cheers."

I hung up the phone and fell back asleep. When I woke up the sun was down and the clock was flashing 12:00. I guess someone fixed the electricity.

I decided that I wanted to get dressed up for dinner since I had felt like trash for the last couple days. The "Euro-trash Girl" song by Chix on Speed kept playing in my head and I begged of it to stop but my head doesn't always listen to me. So I put my hair back and put my makeup on. I slipped into my stockings, form-fitting black skirt, cashmere sweater, and chunky black heels, and I buttoned my mauve velvet jacket. I picked up my wallet, keys, and book of Bukowski from the dresser and I was out the door. I went to the front desk to ask about vegetarian restaurants and they recommended an Indian place. I considered it, but then thought that the spices would definitely be too much for my digestive system. The hotel had an Italian restaurant in the lobby. I decided to go with that.

I walked in. The waiter smiled and asked how many.

"Table for one, please." Table for One would be a great band name. I need another solo project so I can call it Table for One. It would have to be horribly whiney emo-esque songs about broken hearts and self-indulgent pity. The waiter led me to my table and handed me the menu. I perused their selection of pastas, sauces, and vegetables, creating a combination that was vegan and full of as many veggies as I could handle. I decided on penne pasta with a tomato sauce with broccoli and plum tomatoes. The waiter smiled and leaned in close to me. I could feel his warm breath slithering its way down my neck.

"We normally don't make special orders. But for you beautiful, anything."

"Thanks," I said, trying to smile over the turning of my stomach by the waiter's intrusive actions. He was creepy. Well coifed, but creepy nonetheless. Why am I always playing the part of the creepy guy magnet? My magnetism seems to be at its highest magnitude when I'm completely exhausted, when my guard is completely down. The creepy guy circles in on this weakened state like a vulture, waiting for me to let my guard down and then begins to incessantly peck at my unsuspecting flesh.

The waiter returned with the food. Bread, olive oil, and vinegar on a small round plate and a bowl of pasta. I dug in, ravenous from not eating properly for days. The bread and olive oil agreed with my stomach well but the garlicky pasta was questionable. I only ate half and saved the rest for later that night. I've found that cold pasta is often even more flavorsome than warm pasta. It's amazing how that works.

"Can I get a to-go box for the rest? And just bill the meal to room five-fifteen."

The waiter returned with a box, the check, and his number.

"So now that I know what room you're in . . . what if I

stop by in about an hour with a bottle of wine, good wine for you and me, eh?"

"Sorry, I'm exhausted and have to work in the morning. Thanks, though." I didn't have energy to be rude. I went back to my room collapsed after finishing Bukowski's *Women*. I woke up around 6 A.M. and watched the sun rise over the foggy city.

Katrina picked me up as promised and brought me to her dungeon. We had to work quickly, as she had to be back at the house by 3 P.M.—the yellow bus would be pulling up and dropping off her two darling daughters from elementary school. Katrina snugged her body into a black PVC cat suit, threw on her black, bobbed wig to cover her delicate Danish blond locks, and proceeded to tie me with her fine collection of Romanian hemp rope. My hands were tied together and forced upward, suspended from my body toward the eye-hook in the ceiling. The video was rolling and the camera was snapping away. The delicate Danish mother with locks of blond hair had disappeared from existence for this hour; Selina, the dominant mistress of Denmark, reigned over the landscape of my body. Her hands came in delicate, growing in appetite as they stroked and explored my naked body that trembled under her touch. My nipples had grown hard in anticipation of her caress and the bite that I knew would follow. The single tail was one of her specialties. She knew and controlled the implement like it grew out from the tips of her fingers. My body winced in pleasure, drawing itself in and then reaching out for more.

Snap-whisp-whisp-whisp-Snap

Hard against the back, ass, and thighs. Hard, then teasingly with the tip with a cruel tenderness. My body shook and I felt the absence of Gauge. I knew that she was gone. That this was it. That this was final.

Snap-Snap-Snap—hard against the back 'til I thought my body would break in two and
Snap-Snap-Snap-SNAP!

I broke—tears flooding my eyes, sent straight from my gut, running circles around my heart and burning the back of my throat and nose. I was coughing up tears, choking on my own shit. And I became one with the electric lines of pain that ran into and out of my body in zigzags, in beautiful purple, red, and blue. I was part of an electrical storm. I was the lightning and thunder striking hard and I begged for my outsides to hurt as much as I did inside. I wanted to rid myself of an emptiness, and bed with pain and sensation. I would take bruises and marks out to dinner and fuck stings and thuds on the weekends. I would even take pain out for coffee in the morning before I dropped her off at her house hung over and hand-cramped from the way my cunt swallowed her digits.

Snap-Snap-Snap-Crack-Crack-Crack!

My cunt was as wet and sopping as my eyes. And I didn't really remember which one I look both ways with before crossing the street.

She untied my hands and I fell into her breasts as she stroked my hair. My hand petted her thighs instinctually, in the rhythm of my breath, of my hyperventilation. Breathing hard, breathing tears. I wiped my eyes and made my way to the dressing room to put on my clothing and wipe off my makeup.

After the shoot I was off to London with a pocket full of Kroners. My friend Josh had picked up an airline ticket for me so I wouldn't have to deal with the train yet again. As I sat back on the boarding plane, leaning against the lightly chilled window, my cheek grew cold and dead. My mind wondered as my eyelids became heavy with travel and my clit became hard. Airplanes had become a recent fetish for me that left me hard and wet. I was overcome with jet lag and I wanted nothing more than to fall deep into sleep and wake up late in the afternoon to breakfast cooking and someone's warm body wrapped around mine. She'd feel warm and soft and taste like creamsicles and my body would shiver when I'd taste her center. Her thin boney fingers would be full of confidence and desire. They would start a journey at my forehead and press my skull to the bed, dragging their way down my face, squashing my nose in the palm of her hand. I would breathe in deep to inhale the bitter scent of my cunt that resided in the sweat that melted from her hand after spending so much time in my aching cavern. My red lipstick would smear as her hand dragged across my mouth and into and out of my salivous hole. My tongue would swirl circles around her narrow fingers and nibble roughly at her calluses. Her hand would open wide as it slides down to my neck, grabbing, tightening, applying just enough pressure to get my pussy wet and to keep me from breath. My eyes widen as they consume and want for her to be inside of me much greater than I could ever want breath. I start to turn blue and purple and red and wet. Wet should be a color. It would be a beautiful color. I think that would be my favorite color, wet. I turned deep, dark wet and—London hit me with an abrupt landing and I found my way on top of Ruby.

So there I was straddling Ruby Monroe on the leather couch, pumping my hand in and out of her, through her Wolford fishnet stockings. My other hand ran up and down her thigh, grabbing at her ass, occasionally coming up for an over-flowing handful of tit that was more than I knew what to do with. My tongue lapped hungrily at her pussy through her stockings. She had gotten me hungry for her and I could see how hungry she was for me to fill her up. I was up for the challenge. Ruby and I knew one another from our photos, from Web sites and producers we had both worked for. Our images and URLs had been rubbing up against each other's nakedness for years, but it wasn't until now that we had finally come face to face. I was never much into Ruby from her photos. She seemed too typical porn star: tan, huge sili-cone tits, long hair, false lashes, high heels. She was a person-ification of sex or perhaps the exhausted afterglow that appeared postcoitus. Now here I was, in London in a strange house in the wee hours of the after-party morn, fuckin' the shit out of Ruby Monroe while the four or five remaining party guests watched in amazement. The men taking notes and adding commentary, trying to uncover the secrets of women's pleasure making.

"You know what's good about women?" said one of the voyeurs. "Everything."

And I thought. Oh yes. Everything.

I really hadn't planned on fucking Ruby that night or, for that matter, ever. It kind of just happened. If I was a guy, I would use the excuse, "I just tripped and my dick fell in."

I was totally getting off having my hand in her pussy, locating that nice round mound of G-spot and rubbing, pressing, and fucking it. Her pussy was warm and comforting, like being wrapped in a toasty blankie. I just wanted to curl up inside. It had been nearly a month since I had fucked a woman, my Gauge, and I missed women. I needed women. I needed tits and ass and warm pussy. And their smell and their softness, and I needed them.

Ruby had walked in with the editor of *Second Skin Magazine*. I had managed to finish off a bottle of cheap red wine by this point and was feeling socially courageous enough to introduce myself to strangers.

"Hey . . . my name is Madison. We haven't ever officially met or anything but we are on a lot of the same sites together. I just thought I'd come over here and say hi."

"Hi," she said in a high squeaky voice. "It is really nice to meet you. I know who you are. I've been seeing your photos for the last two years."

We sat and talked shop for a minute and then I flitted off. After most the night remaining relatively quiet—with the exception of a discussion on gender identity that I found myself engaged in with a self-identified gender-queer boi—I was now at the point in the night where I wanted to be social. People no longer frightened me or creeped me out. I trusted this small group of people and I was now ready to socially engage. I moved from one group of people to the other, chatting about queer politics and BDSM. I discovered a group of fellow kinky Ohio expats who had found themselves in large cities like LA and NYC and London, but none of us could deny our Ohioian roots. We found our new families buried deep in metropolitan areas thick with smog, club life, and open-minded freaks. We had decided that we were suburban survivors. We had endured growing up in an intensely conservative environment while identifying outside of the available boxes that we were handed as children, and we chose to knock down the picket fences and find greener pastures among skyscrapers and city folk. We were brothers and sisters of a sprawling war of conformity.

Our moment of drunken bonding came to an abrupt halt as the evening's bidding began. This was nothing that was organized, but sort of a spontaneous auction for debaucherous activity.

"Do I hear ten pence for removing of the trousers?"

"I'll pay thirty pence if Midori goes without a shirt the rest of the night."

A shirt flies off

"Fifty pence for Ruby to piss in a teapot."

Pssssss

"Twenty pence if you drink it."

The British gentleman pours a proper teacup of Ruby's piss and swallows.

"My piss tastes really good. It's because I drink a lot of water," Ruby informs the kitchen full of partygoers.

More wine. Must have more wine! I've gotten to the "I'm trashed" part of the evening, when more alcohol must always be in my cup. I drank large mugs full of the red fermented grape divinity. I swirled the intoxicating liquid around in my mouth and felt the warmth of the room slide down my throat as I swallowed.

I found my way over to Ruby. We were only talking, but she kept talking so very close, and her lips seemed to be just right there, and then closer and closer and boom—the lips were off. Racing and wrestling with each other. She kept wanting more. She seemed like this enormous canyon of want and loneliness that needed to be filled and I tried to fill the gap, working hands over flesh, tongues wrestling, lips biting and dancing with all of the want and loneliness. She seemed so lonely. So removed. It made me sad. I kept on. The center of the party gravitated to our lips.

"Wow! Did anyone here see that coming?"

"Grab them!" someone yelled.

Someone parted us and picked Ruby up, and another guy picked me up. They threw Ruby on the leather couch and threw me right on top of her. We continued without a hitch, but now our hands roamed free and skirts hiked upward and teeth bit into flesh and kept going and going until finally her ride had to leave and we exchanged numbers.

"Call me," she said. "You're fun, I like you."

I felt so male in her presence. I wasn't used to such a femme—a true femme whose interest and business was all about enhancing, maintaining, marketing, and selling her femaleness. I stumbled back to the place I was staying at, only a couple blocks from the party. My first night in London and I'm already finding myself in compromising positions, belligerently drunk and fucking a girl that I just met. I sure know how to break in a city.

Prospects or Bust

Alex Zephyr

Sauntering down the boardwalk blanketed with cracks and embedded with wavering rivers crisscrossing, Marina stuffed her hands in her tattered jeans pockets. Her fingers, chilled and shriveled, rubbed against rusty pennies, paper scraps, and receipts bloodied with dark ink. Billowing gray clouds swirled in giant masses above, exerting water droplets, sized equal to that of a quarter. The rain seemed relentless. Palm trees planted in eleven-foot intervals surrounding the walkway swayed dramatically, their ruffled leaves courting all who wandered underneath. The wind was harsh and unwelcoming.

Enthralled by the lifestyle of squatting, Marina had run away at fourteen. Her father left the family when she was seven. Her mother, an avid cokehead and alcoholic, had resigned her card as a single mother of two by marrying a sixty-four-year-old man, whose prowess in the art of fist and metal on his stepkid's skin had led to the permanent AWOL of Marina and her brother. Marina's brother, Tristan, was a year and one month younger than Marina and in light of his escape and newfound life on the streets had been easily coerced by a fellow squatter to enter the sex work business. He was arrested on Marina's sixteenth birthday, while participating in a drug deal in Albuquerque, New Mexico, and was sentenced to two years in a juvenile rehabilitation facility located in Paris—Paris, Texas.

After his arrest Marina had continued to train-hop for a year or so, squatting in parts of New Mexico, Arizona, Nevada, Oregon, and California. Marina had settled in San Francisco however, making Golden Gate Park her primary place of residency. Grief stricken by the thought of her kid brother re-entering society (he had been a resident of the rehab program for a year and eight months, by this time) only to continue subjecting himself to a life of dope and prostitution, Marina planned to seek out a person who would willingly offer her a place to live. She would stay there temporarily, at least until she had saved enough money to rent out a place in the Bay Area. To fill the prerequisite of the court, so that Tristan may reside with Marina in a safe and stable environment following his sentence, she must have paid two months, rent and have an open room for him, by his release date.

Marina extended her ripped shoe into a bed of icy liquid, which ran swiftly parallel to the sidewalk. She let out a sigh, then reared her body, lifting her back foot off of the curb, stepping into the street. Angry puddles grew and threw themselves at her.

Marina curved to the left, sloshing beneath the overhang of Destiny Bean. The luminous "We're Open" sign was flickering with brilliant rays of neon flashing, on, off, on, off. Marina pulled her hands from the drenched abyss of her pockets and ran them across her dirt-smeared face, then through her hair.

"Gawd, I wanna cut this off," she muttered, touching the nape of her neck, where her soggy brown hair ended. Marina stepped forward slightly, standing beside a small marble table, equipped with a centerpiece, a single ashtray. She reached down and gripped the metal frame of a chair, pulling it until its backing pressed against her thighs. She sat, facing the interior of the coffee shop, listening to the whooshing of cars whizzing past. The torrential rain was still slicing down like razor blades, feverishly as ever. Marina read a notice taped to the window, a paper she had glared at so many times before. It read: Our Tables Are Reserved For Our Patrons. We Reserve The Right To Refuse Service To ANYONE. *That's crap*, thought Marina, as she peered through the coffee shop window. *If I could pay every time I came around here I sure as hell would, but I can't. How the fuck is a kid like me supposed to eat if she has to barf up cash for coffee every damn day? Whatever. It's not gonna matter anymore. Once I find a place to stay. . . .* Marina squinted her eyes, peering through the coffee shop's window and scanned the faces of those she could manage to see inside, searching for some sort of familiarity. Two butch women, both dressed in surf brand-name hooded sweatshirts and board shorts were in the process of eating a plate of pita, hummus, and sliced cucumbers. A gangly woman stood impatiently, near the end of the counter, tapping her freshly manicured nails on her neatly ironed jeans. The man behind the counter wore a plain black T-shirt; his face told her that he had a load of other places he'd rather be.

Marina clamped her eyelids shut and shivered, wishing that she had enough for a cup of joe. She knew that she did not, for she had counted her change only fifteen minutes before, calculating her total: four dimes, a nickel, and eighteen pennies. Altogether, that was sixty-three cents, sixty-two cents short for a small cup of coffee. Marina sat, thinking about how wonderful it would be if she randomly discovered a dollar bill or a few quarters in one of her pockets. This thought rested upon her brain, jeering at her, forcing her to dive her hands back into her pockets, to search. Just as her fingertips reached the bottom of the damp cloth, the door of the shop swung open.

"Ding-ring-ding!" sang the antique metal bell tied to the handle of the door. Marina's head jerked up, in reaction to the abrupt sound.

The silhouette of a woman appeared several feet in front of Marina. She stepped forward, slowly, the "Open" sign illuminating her face. Her shirt had "Destiny Bean" written on it, as well as the coffee shop's logo, two animated coffee beans standing on a winding road. *She's probably going to bitch about me sitting out here and tell me to leave*, thought Marina. *I might as well get up and go now, so that I won't have to listen to her!* Preparing to walk away for the table, away from the figure, Marina stood up.

"Naw, it's alright, I don't bite or anything, relax, stay for a little," said the woman, chuckling. "I mean, if you want to. . . . I just came out here for some fresh air." She took a pack of Lucky Strikes out of her jacket pocket and held them up to show Marina, who slowly dropped back into the chair. "You do know it's *raining*?" asked the woman dramatically. Marina knew she was joking and did not find the comment funny at all, but she laughed, sorely out of sympathy.

"Hey, mind if I sit here?" inquired the woman. Marina's head wavered from side to side, signifying that she did not.

What the hell am I getting myself into? she questioned herself. The young woman held two equal-sized paper cups. She rested the cups atop the table, pulled up a chair, then sat. She then pulled a cigarette out from the pack, setting it delicately between her full lips. Marina cocked her head to the left, shifting her gaze to the flooded street. *What is this lady doing?* she wondered. Marina heard the clicking of a lighter, then glanced up, observing the woman's cheeks expand then compress.

"Want a smoke?" the woman asked, dropping the pack on the table beside the lone ashtray. Marina did not respond, or move. She could not believe that this person was treating her so kindly. She was used to people approaching her with words of angst and utter disrespect; either that or no words at all. Marina felt lost and overwhelmed by this stranger's words and actions.

"Kid, it's cold as hell out here! And you're soakin'!"

Marina took a breath, inhaling the woman's distinct fragrance, the combination of patchouli and smoke. "My name's Jordan. I work here." Marina did not recall ever seeing this woman before, and figured she must have been hired recently. "Want one?" Jordan nodded down, to portend that she was referring to the cups of coffee. Jordan paused, as if she were waiting for Marina to speak.

"Pitter, patter," replied the rain, thumping against the top of the plastic overhang.

"It's organic," Jordan went on, more excitedly, "but it's flaming hot, so careful." Jordan slid one of the cups toward Marina. Marina felt the steam exerted by the hot substance, kiss her cheek. She wanted the coffee desperately but did not trust Jordan and did not want to feel as though she was required to talk.

"No. Thanks, though. I'm alright," Marina said.

"Don't be a martyr, c'mon, take it! I want you to know that I just want to talk with you. See you here all the time and I'm only trying to be friendly. If I intruded, I'm sorry. If I made you uncomfortable I didn't mean to. I just figured you wanted . . ." Her voice trailed off.

Marina's face flushed, she tried to respond, but it felt like her tongue were swollen, a massive beast within the tiny cave of her mouth. Her body became stiff, preventing her from executing any motion besides that of slumping farther in the rickety, metal-plated chair. She was rapidly shifting her jade tinted eyes to trace Jordan's visage.

Should I just take the damn coffee? If I do she'll probably leave. I won't have to talk to her. And she won't see how stupid I am, Marina wondered.

"You have a name?" Jordan asked, grinning. Marina flushed with embarrassment and nervousness, she felt giddy. This was strange to her. She couldn't understand why Jordan was still there, talking to *her!* "I've seen you here before, but whenever I do, you're writing away, and I never want to interrupt. . . ." Marina's face grew hot. Jordan swiftly turned her body around watching the road with her intensely brown eyes. Marina thought Jordan saw her embarrassment, turning as if to give her a moment to re-dress and collect herself. She shrugged, rolling her eyes within malice sockets. *What the hell!*

"Marina."

"Nice to meet you, Marina." Jordan said, reaching out her hand. Marina shivered and eyed Jordan's nails, bitten raw. Marina extended her hand cautiously, only to retreat it after only a split second of contact. She clenched her fists, then drew them beneath the circular table. Her insecurity was a constricting bandana wrapped around her head. It seemed to be preventing her from exercising both sight and sound.

"So you write? Awesome. I'm a painter myself. It takes all the tension of working at this hellhole away." Jordan sucked on her cigarette, looking intrigued. "How long have you been writing?"

"Um . . . " Marina felt naked. Jordan was stripping down all her defenses and Marina had no idea how she was supposed to act, what she was supposed to do or say. She bent her head and ran her tongue across her lips, dry and cracked, faintly tasting blood.

"You don't have to answer. I was only wondering."

"Since I left my house, I guess. About three years . . . yeah."

"Writing is your release, then?"

"Yeah, somethin' like that." Marina drank her coffee in unheard slurps, while Jordan put out her cigarette in the cheap plastic ashtray.

"Huh, that's interesting. Words never did much for me. I'm not illiterate or anything, don't get me wrong, I guess I just never developed that skill. You know, uh, what is it called?" Jordan reached for her pack of Lucky Strikes, preparing to smoke another. "Oh! Painting a picture in the reader's mind. Yeah, I seem to create more with pastels and paints than with words or metaphors."

Marina was beginning to feel a little more comfortable. She was captivated by her new acquaintance.

"Shit! No fuckin' way, it's already nine-thirty!" Jordan proclaimed as she stood up abruptly, her thighs bumping the table. Marina reached with both hands to steady the wobbling paper cups, half full with tepid coffee. In vain, she struggled to set the cups upright, until both hers and Jordan's fell to the wet concrete ground below. The warm substance secreted the strong scent of organic coffee, setting the perfect tone for Jordan who continued to speak.

"My breaks always end as quickly as they begin. I'm so sorry about the coffee spillage." Jordan pointed her nail-bitten index finger at a beige stain on Marina's jacket, and smiled. "Hey listen, I'd really like to talk some more about you and your writing. What do you think, tomorrow, perhaps? I close again, so I'll be here around three o'clock or a little before."

Marina almost wanted Jordan to invite her to her house. The more she thought about going home with this woman, the more she considered Tristan and how much he needed her to be there for him. *It's better that I don't fuck anything up now. I'll just tell her a little more about myself tomorrow, and hopefully she's let me sleep on her couch or refer me to someone with more resources,* she thought.

"Yeah, sounds good, I'll be around. It's not like I live miles away. Hell"—Marina shrugged her shoulder and looked around—"I could pitch tent anywhere, the windmill, the beach, the park, an alley off Hyatt, wherever."

"Well, take care of yourself, Marina." Jordan flashed another smile and, picking up the dripping coffee cups, entered the door to the Destiny Bean, to finish up that night's work, leaving Marina enveloped by a misty silence blanketing the front patio.

Stay

Beth Steidle

Desire is stressful. This I have learned from my mother, my mother who, if she can find the bed, passes out beneath a thin, gold crucifix. Desire is worthless. This I have learned from my grandmother, eyes staring down a massive silver pot on an electric stove. Desire is suicide. This I have learned from my brother, body sprawled across the train tracks, hands wet with the gutted deer. Desire is nicotine. This I have learned from my grandfather, one lung removed and sent by doctors to die in the countryside.

Nicotine is desire is desire is nicotine. The principles of the cigarette ratio. In the end, it will all come down mathematically, x and y variables, nicotine, desire, and a single inverse line.

There are two women in this story, sucking down cigarettes to keep hands and mouths occupied. One is half empty, the other half full. It doesn't really matter which one is which, but for the sake of narrative, I will be the one half empty. Look, there I am, starting inside out: two ovaries, shrinking stomach, two miles of intestines, lungs going black, one heart, and one brain. Dyed black hair, pale skin, the diagram of a heart tattooed on a chest.

She's the one with her legs collapsed beneath her, long spindle arms falling straight down from sockets to a puddle on the floor. She is painful to look at. The fact that she is beautiful is a lie and a truth, and beautiful is the wrong word for the wrong gender.

She yawns across the blue hibiscus. Beneath the lamplight her ribs are albino/black/albino/black and I watch the shadows cross into her hollows, the shadows like Rorschach tests and I turn them into hands, my hands, my black hands, up and down the length of her spine.

No, never mind. My hands are in my lap, then crushed between the weight of my thighs, where I tell them to stay. It is strange the way my hands act beneath the pressure of the better part of my brain. I will say *stay* and they will say *go,* I will say *stay* they will say *go.* Stay go stay go stay go, hands. Breathe, drink, eat. Hands. Stay.

Stay, she says. This is your house where will you go?

Then get out of my house, I say.

Never mind, there are three women in this story. One fills the second who tries to fill the third who empties the first. I am the first, she is the second, the third is the third.

This is the part of the story where she goes home to find the third woman, the one she is trying to stop desiring. The third woman balled up on the couch, a strange curl of beauty. The third woman reflected a thousand times in the blue spheres slung on the fir tree in the corner, coated in spastic white lights. This is the part of the story where my lover sees herself slumped on the eye-whites of her former lover and her former lover has become a thousand blue women with glass hips. This is the part where she touches them all.

Stay, the second says.

This is my house, the third replies. *Get out.*

This is my house too, the second says.

Then don't stand in front of me, the third says.

This is the part of the story where she slams the door of her own house, slinks down into the subway, and comes up in my skin. The doors open, she exits my mouth, she slides her body across the blue hibiscus, the blue hibiscus is an ugly pattern on a carpet I have stolen, and everything in my room is stolen because I am twenty years old.

She slides her skin for miles, through beer bottles filled with cigarettes sucked to the filters, soaking in stale water. The landscape of fiber and glass and skin. I mark the valley between the base of her ribs and her pelvis, a dark place. It would be nice to live there, perhaps I will build a small house out of her bones. It will be shaped like a martyr.

Stay, this is your house, where will you go?

On a certain Sunday of a certain month with a certain brand of credit card, admittance to the aquarium is free. That is where I go. Red line to blue line, get off at the stop marked Aquarium, slide the card beneath the pane of glass that separates us, the attendant looks bored, prints out a slip, here you go, I go.

They put the penguins at the entrance because those birds are social. They are shitting everywhere, shitting and shitting. They won't stop. Everyone seems to love this.

Avoid the crowds, head toward the tanks. Everywhere is light cast through water, cast into air. If you were me, you would feel like you are drowning. You would watch the water coat your skin, you would look up through miles and miles of salt and hydrogen and oxygen and transparent fin and electric bulb.

Her skin is so thin, I can see right through it. She becomes hibiscus, she fades, she blurs. This is how memory works. She fades into my father, my mother, my brother, my hometown, somewhere New York. My stars, my gardens, my hemlocks, my locusts. My exoskeletons hung all over. She fades until she hums like a filament and the sound is so constant I stop hearing it.

The octopus is cupped, liquid skulled and eight legged in the corner of his glass case. He does nothing, the children stare wide-eyed and fearful. His presence is cruel, and obscene in its ugliness.

No, never mind. She clots into my skin like an angry welt and I am blind, asking to be blindly held. This I have learned from the darkness: arms are arms, if you leave before sunrise no one is worse off.

This is the part where someone says, *Come over* and I say, *Okay*. This is the part where he says, *Drink whiskey* and I say, *Okay*. This is the part where he says, *Write poetry* and I say, *Okay*. He says, *Kiss me* and I say, *Okay*. He has nothing in his room except for a typewriter and a vase of white flowers and a music box. I turn the key and the notes play and the ceramic dancers go and go in circles and their gaze is steady and they are male/female/male/female in perfect orbit.

The shark swims lazily, some fish swim lazily, the starfish sit and observe, some have five legs, some have four. Some fish eat other fish and the other fish sit there and take it.

I leave his house before sunrise, I go red-line, red-seat back home to my stolen apartment where the walls are paid for but the insides are not. I sit in the same place. She shows up with a six-pack on a Sunday. She wonders if I have moved and when she asks I will say, *Nope*.

She drinks like a fish, we sit there and take it. I don't drink but I will on special occasions. She forgets about my medications and lets me do it. She hands me the bottle like it is a casual gift and I say, *Thank you.* No, never mind, I don't say anything at all.

Silence, silence, until the sun sets and the lamp is on but flickering and unstable and it looks like water and I lie in it and I bathe in it and I wash myself in light, come out clean, by which I mean drunk.

I say, I am a dismembered starfish.

I actually say this, and cannot believe I am saying it even as I do, and she does not blink once, only says, *Okay.* I say this and I actually mean it, my legs are numb and I cannot feel anything. There are pleasantries and millimeters between us.

I did not come here so you could sit here like this and act like I've been nothing to you, she says.

Then leave, I say.

Stay, my hands say.

Desire is stressful, desire is worthless, desire is suicide. Desire is isolation and self-isolation is not a disease. This I have learned from my father, the once-psychologist who waltzes with hemlocks. My memories of these men, these women, stand like perfect porcelain figures and when I turn the key they orbit my eyes. She is dancing now, too, fading into a figure I have molded.

These figures do not actually exist, they are only bodies I have filled with music. They are beautiful in stillness and beautiful in movement and their smiles are red-etched on white faces. I have eliminated the awkwardness of human existence, the red greyhound veins, the torn vocal chords, the branch my mother swung at me because I did not come when I was called, and we were supposed to be going to So-and-So's swimming pool. But I am not powerful, I am drunk.

I slump onto the carpet which is stolen onto the floor which is paid for. She asks me what I have done to chemicals in my head. I say, *No, what the chemicals have done to me*. She hands me my pills, they swarm across the synapses like chemical egrets, her hand touches mine and I say, *Stay*. I say *stay* with both my hands and my mouth.

About the Contributors

Page McBee is not a big fan of gender and would rather you think of her as not having one. Originally from Pittsburgh and Boston, she is a writer, teacher, and events organizer. She has performed her work at the Radar Reading Series in San Francisco, LitQuake in San Francisco, Homo a Go Go in Olympia, K'vetsh (San Francisco, Boston, and Pittsburgh), Brown University, and Sarah Lawrence College, among others. She is the co-founder and curator of K'vetsh-Pittsburgh, the former co-host of K'vetsh-Boston, and she currently co-curates a multimediate collaborative events series in San Francisco called "Go." Page is a graduate student in Fiction at San Francisco State University and endlessly working on her memoir hybrid, *The Milkman Theory*.

Zoe Whittal is the author of the forthcoming novella/short fiction collection *Bottle Rocket Hearts* (Cormorant Books), and a poetry book called *The Best Ten Minutes of Your Life* (McGilligan). She edited the short fiction anthology *Geeks, Misfits and Outlaws* (McG), and her prose and poetry have been anthologized widely in books like *Brazen Femme:*

Queering Femininity (Arsenal Pulp), *Breathing Fire 2: Canada's New Poets* (Nightwood Editions), and *Girls Who Bite Back* (Sumach Press). She is currently working on a second book of poetry called *The Emily Valentine Poems,* and, with artist Suzy Malik, a graphic novel about a tomboy femme eight-year-old with superpowers. She makes her living as a freelance book reviewer and publicist for Toronto-based independant feminist publishers. You can read more about her at www.tla1.com.

Claudia Rodriguez is a writer/activist from Compton, California. She received her MFA in creative writing from the California Institute of the Arts (CalArts). Her work has appeared in *Blithe House Quarterly, Chicana/Latina Studies: The Journal of MALCS, Trepan, Tongues Magazine, The Los Angeles Gay and Lesbian Latino Arts Anthology,* and *Westwind: A Journal of Critical Studies,* out of UCLA. Claudia received an Emerging Lesbian Writer award from the Astraea Foundation in 2001. She has taught at Loyola Marymount University and UCLA, and she is a founding member of Butchlalis de Panochtitlan, a sketch-driven performance/installation/video ensemble.

Amanda Davidson is a San Francisco–based writer and multimedia artist.

Sloane Martin is currently a senior at School of the Arts High School in San Francisco, majoring in creative writing. She has been published previously in the SOTA Creative

Writing department's literary journal *Umläut,* as well as the literary journal *Instant City* and has two self-published chapbooks. For hate mail, love mail, or any other kind of mail, e-mail her at eightiesbaby89@yahoo.com.

Dexter Flowers is a Portland, Oregon–based writer. She spends most of her time digging up awkward stories from her childhood, reveling in fantastical eccentricities and sentimental moments, running away with the circus, and making her comic book, *my red umbrella.* She also has a new zine of memoirs called *Maybe It's Something You Ate.* Dexter hosts spoken mics in Portland and is secretly working on a book about growing up with a single mom in an alternative household and the various father figures that came along the way.

Katie Fricas has only just begun making comix. When she is not flip-flopping between jobs as a waitress and a secretary she is teaching herself to draw and reading lots of books. Her strip *Dismal Devin* was recently published in the comix anthology *Juicy Mother 2: How They Met* (Soft Skull Press). Her other titles include *Scumby Baby* and *Pigeon.* Some of her work can be found at www.profanescrod.com.

Jenna Henry was born in Winter Park, Florida, and currently lives in San Diego. Her interests include: the smell of gasoline, Diet Pepsi, deep-sea creatures, trashy places and people, women, makeup, dreaming, travel, and Scrabble. Or Travel Scrabble. Where she sees herself in five years: writing books and short stories, running or jaywalking the streets trying to figure out where to go, falling recklessly in love, and getting better at math (or meeting someone who can add things up for her).

Tamara Llosa-Sandor is a twenty-five-year-old Filipina Jewish Whitegirl, born and raised in her much-beloved state of California. She now lives in self-exile in the puritanical wilds of New England, finishing her B.A. in American Studies at Smith College. Besides writing, Tamara can often be found lying out in the sun doing a sudoku puzzle or enjoying a bowl of ramen while listening to Kiss's *Double Platinum* on her new suitcase player.

Meliza Bañales is a writer originally from Los Angeles. She is the author of *Say It With Your Whole Mouth* (Monkey Press, 2003), and her work has been featured in *Lodestar Quarterly, Transfer,* and *The Lesbian News* and in the anthologies *Revolutionary Voices* (Ami Sonny, Ed., 2000) and *Without A Net: The Female Experience of Growing-Up Working Class* (Michelle Tea, Ed., 2004)—both of which were Lambda Literary Award Nominees. She is the 2002 Oakland, California Grand Slam Poetry Champion, the first Latina to win a poetry slam championship on the West Coast, and the 2002 winner of the People Before Profits Poetry Prize. Her second book of poems, *51 Poems About Nothing At All,* is forthcoming, as are her entries for the first *Encyclopedia of Activism and Social Change* (Sage Press) Her poem "Do The Math" is being made into a short film by Mary Guzmán. She lives in San Francisco.

When not slinging drinks, **Jess Arndt** spends her time awash in tales of the sea, sailors, and assorted buggery. Currently completing her MFA in Fiction from Bard College, she has most recently been published in *On Our Backs Magazine, Velvet Mafia: Dangerous Queer Fiction, Instant City Journal,* and *Bottoms Up!: Writing About Sex* (Soft Skull Press). She is wrestling her first novel, a high-stakes adventure story set in 1850s Barbary Coast San Francisco.

Rhiannon Argo is a writer and future progressive librarian. Her stories have been published in *Lowdown Highway* (Junkyard Books), *Transfer Magazine,* and in her own handmade chapbooks. She has a degree in Creative Writing from San Francisco State University, was a committee member for Project Queer Lit, and has organized various literary events in San Francisco. She is passionate about four-letter words and on an average day may have a few scrawled on her hand, so as not to lose track of future character names. She is also a firm believer in what one might call "good ole fashioned ladies room gossip" and can justify an overexposure to this sort of activity as a primary source of writing inspiration.

Nicole J. Georges is a twenty-five-year-old zinester and illustrator from Portland, Oregon. Her zine, *Invincible Summer,* was recently published as an anthology through Tugboat Press. In the meantime, she is working on a children's book, stitching stuffed animals, and living with too many dogs in her tiny, taxidermy-rich home.

Robin Akimbo is an active writer and performer whose raw talents were first birthed in Montreal but have spread along the East Coast and down the West. Back home she was a prominent member of "Coco Cafe" (performance poets of color) and hosted her own queer/feminist literary soiree, "Deliverance." She figured out how to go to school in America and graduated from the Experimental Performance Institute at New College of California. She has read regularly at events around the Bay Area and recently acted in the Ghosttown Production "AIDS: The Made For TV Musica." Her most ambitious endeavor to date was writing and performing her own one-woman musical, *I'll Tell You Why*, as part of the Fury Factory Festival at the TJT. She loves painting, karaoke, and the dance floor, and wishes she could live everywhere.

Mecca Jamilah Sullivan is from Harlem, New York. She is currently working on her M.A. in English/Creative Writing at Temple University, where she holds the University's Future Faculty Fellowship in Fiction and was awarded the William Gunn fiction-writing award. Her short stories have appeared in *BLOOM* magazine and in literary publications from Temple, Columbia, and Yale Universities. She also has a short story in *What I Know is Me*, a forthcoming anthology of writings by young black women to be published by Harlem Moon/Doubleday in spring 2006. She's currently working on her first novel, tentatively titled *She Woke Up With the Words in Her Mouth*.

Chelsea Starr is a writer and dj living in San Francisco, where she also makes clothes and acts in movies. She used to write poetry and once won $500 in a poetry contest (hate to brag!), but now she sticks to autobiographical fiction. She throws the really fun queer dance party, Hot Pants, and has a chapbook entitled *Long Walks on the Beach with Chelsea Starr.*

San Francisco native **Gina de Vries** was born in 1983. She is the co-editor of *[Becoming]: Young Ideas on Gender, Identity, and Sexuality* (Xlibris Press, 2004). Gina has had her journalism, memoir, fiction, and smut printed various places, including *That's Revolting!: Queer Resistances to Assimilation* (Soft Skull Press, 2004), *On Our Backs* magazine, *Curve* magazine, and *fULL* zine. She has curated performances for San Francisco in Exile, posed for NoFauxxx.com and Come-Together.Be, and archived pornography for the Center for Sex & Culture. She welcomes correspondence at queer-shoulder@gmail.com.

Basking in the trenches of leftover teen angst and an impure agenda, **Cristy C. Road** romanticizes the underdog like it's nobody's business. Cristy C. Road has been illustrating ideas, people, and places ever since she learned how to hold a crayon. Taking the rabble-rouser seriously enabled Road to make it this far as an illustrator, publisher, and writer. At the tender age of 23, her repertoire consists of 10 years of zine publishing; an illustrated novel, *INDESTRUCTIBLE;* and countless illustrations for punk rock bands, political organizations like the CIW and INCITE, and magazines like *Bitch, Jane, Left Turn,* and *The Progressive.* C. Road lives under a live fast dichotomy. In her eyes, there certainly isn't enough one can do before their 25th birthday.

Shoshana von Blanckensee is a Bay Area native who stumbled into writing crappy poetry in her teen years and was then dragged out of college and away on the debaucherous 1998 Sister Spit tour, forever sealing her fate. She is currently in her hundredth year of the MFA creative writing program at San Francisco State. She has been published in a handful of anthologies, and was the recipient of the William Dickey Fellowship in Poetry in 2003.

Jenny Lowery grew up in a small working-class town in southwest Washington. She currently lives in Seattle, where she is a student and board member of the Bent Writing Institute. She is working on a novel about hobo culture. This is her first time published.

Tina Butcher is a queer, sexpositive writer for such magazines as *On Our Backs, Bitch, Herbivore, Skin Two,* and *Girlfriends.* She is currently finishing her first novel, *The Tail of a Bondage Model.* Tina is also a visual artist who shows at galleries in San Francisco, Seattle, NYC, and LA and currently has an exhibition touring with The Traveling Erotic Art Show. When she is not creating art or writing, she is either running the Femina Potens Art Gallery (www.femina potens.com) or getting tied up in her as a bondage model—

a career that lands her all over the world in beautiful and compromising positions that end up in magazines, videos, and on Web sites such as her own: www.madisonbound.com.

Alex Zephyr is a native San Diegan who lives for her involvement in local activism and womyn-run lit events. She enjoys saving the world one werewolf at a time and would rather get married than pay $30,000 to attend a college of any prestige.

Beth Steidle has a B.F.A. in Writing, Literature and Publishing, and greatly recognizes both the value and nonvalue of such a thing. She lives in sometimes Pittsburgh, sometimes New York, sometimes Boston, and sometimes the middle of the desert in the great American Southwest. She hopes to live somewhere new sometime soon. You can read her work in the anthology *Red Light: Superheroes, Saints and Sluts* (Arsenal Pulp Press), and see her art in *Unicorn Mountain,* a lovely independent Pittsburgh publication. Please contact her at Beth_Steidle@hotmail.com, should you feel so compelled. Brutal criticism and simple hellos are more than welcome. And thank you to both Albert French and Michelle Tea for all their support.

About the Editor

M ichelle Tea is the Lambda Award–winning author of *Valencia, Chelsea Whistle, Rent Girl* (with illustrations by Laurenn McCunbin), and most recently *Rose of No Man's Land*, among others. Tea is the co-founder of the San Francisco–based, all-girl spoken word troupe Sister Spit and is also curator of the monthly Radar Reading series at the San Francisco Public Library. She lives in San Francisco.